Delight!
Father, Creator, Spirit

by
Deborah Lamoreaux

Assuming the form of the one Legion called Svikari, in the blink of an eye, Archangel Michael appeared in New York City once more.

Anxious to see her again, he walked quickly. Turned the corner that took him onto the street with the quaint little sidewalk café, where he'd first begun to look forward to his morning meetings with one of the NYPD's finest – Detective Danielle Almonzo.

"Detective," he nodded in greeting as she looked up.

"Hey Svik, what's shakin'? Got something new for me on your former colleagues?"

"No." He pulled out a chair and sat down opposite her. He met her gaze with deepest sincerity. "I actually just wanted to tell you…what a true pleasure it is to see you, up and around again, so soon after that horrific attack on your life."

"A pleasure? Again? Really? I'm still betting you don't even really know what that means, do yuh

Svik?"

He gave her his trademark blank look because he knew how much it amused her.

She shook her head with a smile, her glossy curls bouncing on her shoulders. "But thanks, all the same. It's great to be back. Such a blessing." She took a sip from her cup and then eyed him again as her beautiful face lit with a wide grin.

"What…? Don't tell me…" He allowed the left side of his mouth to quirk upward just a bit, to engage her.

She'd been blessed by the Creator with a unique, singular, and astute wit. Just one of the many things he loved so much about her.

"You have yet another round of humor you'd like to subject me to, this fine morning, is that it?"

She shook her head slowly.

"No? Hmm… Curious." Almost disappointed, but not quite, he turned to look at the electronic newsfeed he pulled up on his timepiece.

"Now, you and I both know there's no need for me to try to get you to laugh anymore."

"Oh really? And why pray tell is that?" Mildly intrigued, he still didn't look up from the screens he'd opened, just yet.

"Because that was you, wasn't it?"

He stopped and eyed her. "I beg your pardon?"

"The angel I saw when I was on the ground in front of the International Center, just bleeding out, and thought I was dying? That was you. And I finally got a real honest-to-goodness smile out of you. Hell, forget that. You nearly busted your gut laughing! I knew I'd get you eventually. I did it. I actually won!

Come on just get it over with and admit it. I know you want to. I got you good, my angelic friend… For real." She made a circle with her forefinger then pointed it at his nose, "*I. Saw you,* and the really crazy thing is, I didn't even plan it, when I made that last joke. It just kinda popped into my head. I think… Can't even recall what it was. Or most of what happened after I got shot, come to think of it. It's so strange… I know it must have hurt like hell, but I can't really remember any of that."

She got those tiny creases in her forehead, above her cute, little nose that he'd noticed she got whenever she was mad or lost in thought.

He got set to add a few more.

"So let me get this straight. You think you saw me?"

She nodded.

"When you thought you were dying?"

She nodded again.

"What was I wearing?" He leaned back and extended his leg out to the side of her chair, to distract her.

"Uh…" Her gaze took a scenic route. From his neck, across his chest, down his leg, to his shoes, and right back up again.

"Well…of course you didn't look like you do normally." She waved an open hand over him. "You were all glorious and bright, and angelic-like, with huge wings and everything. But I do remember hearing *your* voice." She pinned him with her clear gaze. "I'd know it anywhere. God knows, I've heard it enough," she snorted, "that deep, rich, velvet over gravel…mmm…just an acoustic thirst-trap. Kinda like Joe's, only with an accent… *Dang*…" She got a faraway look in her eyes as she bit her lower lip. "Just makes yuh wanna–"

"Ah-hem!" He cleared his throat. "And how *IS* your husband today, Detective?" He gave her a pointed look.

"He's just fine…thank you." She looked confused for a second, then her eyes widened. "Come on now Svik… It's true. I am still blissfully married. Bless God. But that doesn't make me deaf, blind, *AND* stupid!" She burst out laughing and clapped her hands together once. "Ooo-wee, I swear, I crack myself up sometimes. Anyway, you should know me by now…I call 'em, like I see 'em. And you, my friend, are still serving it up. Mm-hmm…" She took him in from head to toe again. "Yes sir, with your *fine* self. What was it you said about me? I'm nothing if not consistent? Well, it's like I told you the first day we met. You'll get no shyness, or subtlety here. Ev-err." She flipped her palms open and shrugged, as she grinned.

He shook his head and sighed, just to give her a little nudge.

"Yeah…uh…so anyway, I know what you did there, yuh know…with the leg, and the husky sighing, and everything. Don't try to distract me." She sat up straighter in her chair and pulled on the corners of her blazer. "Like I said, you know good-and-heaven-well it was you, laughing your head off that day, like there was no tomorrow." She sat forward and pierced him with her pretty hazel-hued gaze, then gasped as she leaned forward even further "And *I* bet you even knew I wasn't actually dying right then, didn't you?"

"And **I**…will not confirm, or deny, any of that." He made his tone dry as he brushed an imaginary speck of dust off the table sitting between them.

"Uh-huh." She tapped her fingernails on it a couple times.

"That's okay," she shrugged and sat back, "because now you know, and I know, that you know, that I know."

"Really? What did any of that even mean? Sounded like a whole lot of nonsense." He raised his left eyebrow.

She didn't respond. Just spread the forefinger and middle finger of her right hand apart, and pointed them at her eyes, and then at his.

She nodded and he almost laughed out loud that time.

Almost.

"Really?" He repeated, as he shrugged instead, and stood.

"Wait," she grasped his arm and looked up into his eyes. "Maybe you're not ready to tell me who you really are just yet, but what about *them*. I'm right, aren't I?" She looked around and lowered her voice, "They are the one third?"

"All in good time, little one." He patted her hand on his arm. "I'll be in touch when I can share more. As always. Do stay safe and blessed, Detective." And like always, he held her gaze just a moment longer than he needed to, as he bestowed his most potent blessing upon her, and her many descendants to come.

"You do the same, Svik."

She released his arm and smiled, and he could see her. Exactly as she would be in the fulness of time. Perfected by the Creator.

And glorious!

With a brief nod, he took his leave. Waited until he cleared the corner, and no one was around, before he disappeared.

He recalled her last thoughts on that fateful day she was shot, very nearly fatally.

Everything that happened.

All of it. In vivid detail.

And the joke too.

"Not afraid of death, but didn't know why the H-E-and-two-sticks she needed to be there when it happened… Now *that*, was a good one." He grinned wide and allowed himself a brief chuckle.

And what a blessing that the Creator had let her retain that bit of their exchange that day. He'd truly enjoyed their little chat that morning. Immensely. His entire being lit up as he praised Him in the moment. Only just recognizing that this and their other encounters were as much a very special gift to him, as they had been episodes of joy for Danielle.

And as always, in His perfect, exquisite timing, exactly what he needed, pouring back into him, right before he rejoined his battalion of angels.

Standing in front of them, he let his light flow from his heart, down his right arm as he swung his mighty sword before him. It flashed like lightning, and they all followed suit. Their light flowing out, one by one, sparking, catching, and spreading, like wildfire across an infinite distance.

Rejuvenated, he turned and looked ahead, into

the gathering darkness.

"Come brothers! With me! For the glory of our Almighty God!"

With a rallying cry that shook the very heavens and every spiritual dominion with the pure power of the Creator, they got set to carry out His holy and righteous bidding.

As they reappeared, in another time, in a dark place…and in a very different dimension…

Chapter 1

Psalms 18:10
And he rode upon a cherub, and did fly: yea, he did
fly upon the wings of the wind…

Marly was in a dark place she just didn't recognize.

Straight ahead…there was no one. No furniture. No windows. Nothing that she could see.

She looked to her left, her gaze drawn like a magnet to the only source of illumination lending relief to the darkness of the space. To a partially open antique door from which white light emanated. It spilled in, brightest at the door, and then grew progressively dimmer as it stretched to the corner she occupied.

She looked down. Realized she was leaning.

On something.

So, the room was not quite as empty as she

thought then.

The solid surface moved a fraction, back and down when she pushed it hard with her hip, but still stayed level, holding quite firm. It was a floating coffee station. Just like the one in the newsroom where she worked. She shifted a bit to her right as she felt the sudden heat of the large steaming, silver urn near her left elbow. She noticed the cups, saucers, and spoons, all metal as well, all around it. All shining in the dim light and laid out in neat lines.

And all at complete odds with the wall behind them.

She took her hip off the counter and turned a bit further to her left. Squinting, as she peered at the wall. Because even in the dimness, there was absolutely no mistaking the disordered, grotesque pattern she could see. Though 'pattern' was probably not the word to use to describe the very random, odd looking, dirty, and dark smears of…

Oh, my dear God…is that–?

"Crap! Is that really you?"

Startled, she jerked forward, away from the counter, and spun to her right.

A man was standing there. In the shadows. Mere meters away.

Unremarkable looking, and casually dressed in dark colored shirt and slacks, he too was leaning, just as she had been, against the front of the beverage station.

"Yeah… I knew you looked familiar." He turned towards her, pointed at her face and nodded. "Didn't think I'd ever see you here again."

She looked around. Her mind in a fog, she tried

to figure out where he could have possibly come from, given the only entrance, or exit she could see, was still on the left. He hadn't made a sound until now. Had he been there the whole time?

And where the hell was she?

And how had she even got there?

"I'm sorry…but do I know you?" She took a step back, away from him.

"Sure. Don't you remember? I saw you the last time. That's how I recognized you right away. Say–" his chin popped up for a second, "–tell me… Exactly *how*…did you die?"

What?!!

He leered at her, his eyes turning a malevolent red.

She very nearly screamed, losing her customary, hard-fought control, as every fiber in her being reacted in urgent alarm, to the real, very tangible, and icy onset of sheer panic. It gripped her by the throat. And was only overshadowed by a sudden and completely irresistible urge to flee.

Heart pounding out of her chest, she heeded that call, turned to her left and ran. Away from the darkness and him, and straight towards the partly open doorway, and to light.

And she prayed to escape.

She yanked it open further, and not looking back for fear of what she might see, she kept on running. Down a long white corridor, for as long as her lungs and legs would allow. Only then did she slow, then stop. She took more than a few deep breaths, put her hands on her hips, looked forward, ahead of her, and hesitantly turned back.

She saw nothing but the seemingly never-ending passageway. Heard nothing, but silence…until…

A word.

She couldn't quite make it out. Soft and indistinct as it was, but sounding like it was coming from…

She turned to her left and suddenly noticed a door, she would have sworn wasn't in that spot in the wall before.

There.

There it was again. As soft as a whisper, but this time she heard it clearly, as it beckoned to her by name.

"Marly…"

Hesitant, she raised her hand toward the door, and it slid open.

And directly ahead, not more than a few meters in front of her, a large picturesque, open window. A wonderful, fragrant breeze wafted across to her, drawing her forward. She took the few steps necessary to get to it, then stood, rested her palms on the sill, and looked out at the most breathtaking view she'd ever seen in her young life.

High overhead, puffy white clouds were scattered across a welcoming powder-blue sky. On the ground below, perfectly sculpted and manicured grounds, with awe-inspiring, towering trees filled her vision. Along with lush green shrubbery, and clusters of colorful flowers of every description, dotted along dozens of neat stone walkways. And at the very center, an extraordinary focal point, too incredible to miss. A magnificent gushing fountain of iridescent water, and of such awesome power, she gasped as her eyes were drawn up and up, as it climbed and then disappeared into the clouds. Leaving multiple tiny rainbows in its wake. Like an honest-to-goodness blessing, returning dutifully to the heavens.

Swish... Swish... SWISH...

Her gaze snapped down, at the sudden sound of powerful, flapping wings, and to her surprise and great delight, three angels floated, mere meters away, in front of her window. Side by side but spaced apart, with exquisite, brilliant white, gossamer feathered wings outstretched so far, they nearly touched.

The one on the left, with hands clasped before him in reverent posture, was praying. The one on the right, also with head bowed, was reading from the good book. While the third, in the very center–

She gasped, as in a flash of light he flew forward, right to her window.

He hovered, nearly nose to nose with her. His eyes – the brightest, truest blue she'd ever seen. His face – a study in manly perfection.

His smile...slow.

"Let it all go...only then can you spread the Word, Marly...and reclaim your joy." His voice, like the rushing of many waters, flowed over, all around, and through her.

He reached out inch by inch, and still holding her gaze, ran his hands from her shoulders right down her arms. He grasped her fingers on the windowsill, and she let out a little shriek, as with a sudden tug, he pulled her out, and high up into the air.

She lost her breath entirely, while he laughed in pure enjoyment, as he held onto her hands and swung her around and around, in a wide circle.

She felt her heart swell, her head just crammed full of giddy gladness.

Every pore of her body tingled as she swirled and twirled in midair, encircled by his contagious, bliss-filled joy, engaged in a dance with him, the wind, and the sky.

And as she closed her eyes and breathed in, deeply, the sweetest, most intoxicating fragrance she'd ever inhaled in her life, she let go of his hands. Surrendered to the leading of her spirit and let out an uncharacteristic shout of gleeful excitement.

She was jolted awake then. To her smile, and to the sound of her own harsh breathing, even as her angel's deep, rich laughter, his heavenly voice, and its rallying call, all still echoed, like beautiful music in her head…

And that was how it all started, just over a year earlier, around her twenty-fifth birthday.

Well, not exactly, since when she'd had those experiences previously, she'd always just believed she was dreaming. Having a really freaky nightmare. Now she recognized her night travels for what they were. Exactly that. Her soul transcending space and time, and moving through another earthbound dimension of reality entirely, only visible to her when she fell asleep.

Preparing for bed, she began her nightly ritual. She walked on bare feet through her apartment to her front door, checked it was locked, and that she'd remembered to set the alarm. Switched on a single light in the passageway outside, and as she made her way back to her bedroom, she pondered her nocturnal trips. Wondered if she'd ever have a normal, decent, uninterrupted night's sleep, ever again.

That first night she came upon her in the hellish realm, she remembered telling her new friend Dani to pray if she couldn't wake herself up. Not because it would bring an end to her torture since in her experience it quite often didn't. But rather because she'd found it to be her only source of strength and real comfort to see her through those inexplicable and disturbing encounters. And indeed, the many trials of her day-to-day life.

She shook her head on a sigh.

Three things at least were for certain, thanks to her experiences, she'd turned a pivotal corner in her faith walk that she might not have otherwise. And for sure, she'd never again be as unprepared around one of those frightening spirits, as she had been before, and on that particular night.

Because thanks to her very heavenly angel…she'd made her third important discovery–

–That wherever, and whenever she wanted… in the very blink of an eye…

She could…

Quite simply…

Fly.

Chapter 2

Proverbs 15:1
A soft answer turneth away wrath: but grievous
words stir up anger...

Time sure did fly.

Marly could hardly believe it had been two months already since she'd met Dani in real life, on the day of that terrible incident.

She got a series of flashes, of the scary man with the gun. The awful, loud explosions. Dani being thrown backward and onto the pavement by the force of the bullets hitting her chest. All the blood. The chaotic scene of by-standers and sky-medic staff gathered around. The shooter being tackled to the ground by police. The way his face, enraged, seemed to shift and change. But surely that was just a trick of shadows and light, and her own worried mind? A nightmare driven manifestation, of the horror enfolding all around her? She shook her head free of the disturbing images.

Now, here she was, at her new friend's stunning home. Truth be told she was thrilled to be anywhere on that Friday night, other than at her own apartment. Alone. Working or watching 21st century programming, as she'd become too well accustomed to doing.

Fortunately, that was her little secret.

"Wow, this place is gorgeous, Dani. Just outstanding." Thinking of what she'd already seen of the sprawling property outside, she looked around the tasteful foyer, with its ultra-modern recessed lighting, and 3-D art pieces. And straight ahead, at a beautiful, antique wooden staircase that led to the upper floors. Everything just added to the nearly perfect blending of modern and classic sophistication.

"Oh, and I couldn't resist picking up some profiteroles for you, from my fave French patisserie. They are amazing! Wait till you taste them. I know you said not to bring anything, but I figured there's always room for more dessert. Am I right?" She handed over the colorful box with a grin.

"Girl, you know it. Thank you so much. That is so thoughtful of you, and thanks again for coming." Dani smiled wide and gave her a warm hug. "Marly, this is my husband, Dr. Joseph Almonzo." She stepped back a bit and turned to her right, where he was standing.

"So nice to meet you, finally." Marly extended her hand to him.

"Same here." He shook it with a warm, firm

grasp.

"Wow…" She looked up and got lost, in the most beautiful, intense, gray-blue eyes she'd ever seen in her life. "Uh…" She raked her mind for something to say to recover from what was surely a gigantic lapse in girlfriend etiquette. "…I've…uh…been following your remarkable career Dr. Almonzo. Your work with stem cell regeneration. It's just phenomenal. Like…wow."

"Thank you, Marly. That's very kind of you to say, but call me Joe, please." He smiled at her, making him even more likeable and gorgeous, if that was even possible.

"Uh…mind if I leave this here?" She broke eye contact with him and turned back to Dani.

"Oh no, sure." Dani nodded, as she unshouldered her handbag, and rested it down on the entryway table.

"Oh, and I believe you already know our newly engaged, phenom financial whiz, Alrissa Cole." Dani pulled her to the left a bit, away from the door, put down the pastries on a side table, and waved a hand towards one of the two people who were already seated close together on a large sofa nearby.

"Of course." She waved. "Hey, Rissa."

"High praise indeed, Dani. Not sure I can live up to that. Hey Marly, great to see you, outside of work." Rissa, the CFO at her media house - Kittridge and Clemens, smiled. Fabulous as usual, in an expensive looking tailored business suit, her long auburn hair was piled up in a chic and fashionable up-do.

"And that's her fiancé over there, and my very

capable boss, the head of NYPD's most elite unit, if I do say so myself, Detective Superintendent Duncan Wright."

"Sure. It's nice to see you again, Detective."

"Call me Duncan, please."

"Okay, thanks."

She smiled.

Nice indeed. She felt more than just a twinge of envy as she took in his casual and rugged, blond good looks, and returned his wave and nod. Both Rissa and Dani were incredibly blessed women, for sure.

"So, did you find the place okay?" Dani touched her arm.

"Oh yeah, I hardly ever drive myself anywhere these days. I just uploaded the coordinates you sent me and let the auto-drive do its thing."

"Uh-huh, hear that, Dani?" Joe chuckled and an engaging smile wreathed his handsome features. He shook his head.

"Oh no, she didn't?" Looking appalled, Dani glanced back and forth between the two of them.

"What?" Marly put a hand to her throat, fingered the tiny crucifix on her chain as she felt the rise of mild alarm.

"Pay no mind to Detective Almonzo here," Joe inclined his head in Dani's direction. "She'd just as soon do a swan dive off a cliff...with no holo-wings...than engage the auto-drive in a vehicle she's travelling in," his lips turned up in a quirky smile. "Makes me drive us manually. Everywhere. Nearly every time we go out."

"*Because*," Dani turned to her, "if you saw the stats that I do, every day, of the number of traffic accidents, injuries and even dismemberments caused by those systems when they malfunction. I'm telling you...*girl*," she grasped her arm and peered at her, her pretty hazel eyes wide, "trust me. It's a dang death trap."

"Okay, Detective," Joe reached out between them. "I think you're scaring our guest. Just walk away, Marly. Just walk away." He chuckled as he clasped Dani's hand between both of his. Dani looked up and glared at him, but then visibly melted as he almost immediately raised it to his lips and placed a single lingering kiss there. Their gazes locked for long seconds.

Feeling awkward as she sensed the tangible heat between them, Marly cleared her throat and added a bright note to her voice. "Okay! I know this is your house, but you two, you really need to get a room already."

"I know, right?" The deep tone of Duncan's voice chimed in from the living room. "I keep telling you Monzo, it's true you guys just recently found each other again, but still, the amount of PDA with you two is just over the top, for real."

"Yeah, yeah, and like *I* keep sayin', why don't yuh stop being such a *love*-party-pooper, and just keep that to yourself, Duncan." Dani licked her top lip without breaking eye contact with Joe, then crooked her forefinger in a beckoning gesture that had him bending his smiling face down to hers to give her not just one, but a series of soft, butterfly kisses this time.

"Okay, so seriously? They're really doing that...like right in front of me?" Marly felt her face heating up as she witnessed their sweet love for each other on full display. "Uh…I think maybe I'll just go freshen up before dinner. Anyone know where the powder room is?" She raised her voice, hoping either Rissa or Duncan would help her out.

Then, looked up, to try to distract herself–

"First time here."

"No clue, sorry."

–And succeeded in ensnaring herself instead. As she stared at the intricate, luminous, and very large, sunken, liquid clock, set deep into almost the entire section of ceiling above her head.

Amazing…

She gaped, as she realized the clock's face was a 3-D illustration, of Christ, sitting in a large ancient wooden ship. It rocked gently, to and fro, at complete odds with the severe turbulence of the dark, churning waters just a small distance away, and surrounding it.

Wait…are those bibles?

Repeatedly he cast out multiple fishing lines with books on the ends, all around the ship and into a sea of people of every gender and ethnicity.

As she watched in awe, some ignored the lines, wrestling instead with the waves as they desperately tried to stay afloat. Some went under. While others caught hold, as though to a prized possession, followed the line with some difficulty, as they navigated the stormy seas between them and the boat. Some let go of the line just at the point where the rough waters intersected with the calm, waded for a while, but were soon drawn backward into the storm. Still others made it through, and victorious, hoisted themselves up at last, into the vessel and safety.

Feeling her eyes tear up, she watched, as wet and bedraggled, some then fell at his feet, while others launched themselves into his welcoming embrace. Over and over the same scenes played out. Yet she felt if given the chance, she could look at it for hours and still see something different. Discover something new, from the very apt and powerful depiction of the human journey of faith.

"Isn't it time…you met the supreme fisher…of men? Time to SURRENDER… To be TRANSFORMED. To DELIGHT yourself in the LORD!" She whispered the inspiring words as she read them off the large inscription clearly visible along the edges of the clock's rippling sides and continued staring.

"It's amazing, isn't it?"

She spun back to the couple, unaware they'd been observing her until she heard Joe's soft question.

"You're telling me. I don't think I've ever seen anything like it. Must be a great conversation starter, huh?"

"Like you wouldn't believe. Speaking of which, what do you think of the message? Does it resonate with you?"

"Oh yeah, absolutely. Well, I think I've got the first two covered, at least. Still, it's a day-to-day process, yuh know? I try to remember to be grateful, for sure. For like, *everything*. But still waiting on the joy part though. Haven't been able to delight myself in much of anything lately."

She thought about her stressful career and her

less than restful nights and stopped herself short of elaborating on just exactly how *undelightful* her life really was at that stage.

"Don't you worry, something tells me your life is about to change. Oh, and the downstairs bathroom is right through there, if you still wanna freshen up before our last guest arrives." Dani raised her eyebrows and pointed to a corridor behind Marly on the right, a short distance past the entryway.

"Oh yeah. Great. Thanks." She nodded as she received the pointed message, then took another last look at the ceiling, "Wow…"

Then she grabbed her handbag, turned about, and headed in the direction Dani indicated.

Marly left the neat, ultra-modern, potpourri-fragrant guest bathroom minutes later, and as soon as she rounded the corner that led back to the entryway, she saw Dani greeting her final guest. The guy she'd said she wanted her to meet.

Facing away from her was a tall, dark-haired man.

Wow…

He had to be at least six foot four…

For her?

Her heart did a little flip in her chest…

Maybe her '*Mr*. Delightful' was arriving sooner than she knew.

Until–

Oh no…

–She'd know those broad shoulders and long legs anywhere.

"Oh, there you are." Dani waved her forward, and he started to turn. "Dax Newton, I'd like you to meet–"

"Marly Sparks," he said with a half-smile as he completed his rotation.

"You?!" She glared at him. Put her hands on her hips, after depositing her bag on the foyer table again.

His left eyebrow popped up, then he scowled.

Of all people. When Dani said she wanted her to meet a nice guy. A good friend of hers and her husband. Why did it have to be him? Her veritable media nemesis, who'd one-upped her on one too many news scoops, and toyed with her tender emotions when she'd been just starting out in her career. So much for thinking she might be meeting Mr. Right here tonight. Typical and just her luck. As if things weren't bad enough, not only did she have to watch both Dani and Rissa spend a blissful night with their ideal significant others, now she'd have to suffer through an entire night near *Mr.* Insufferable, himself.

"You two know each other?" Both Dani and Alrissa asked at the same time. "Jinx!" They shared a grin across the living room.

"Uh…yeah! Unfortunately," she bit out.

Newton leveled a squinting look of disapproval on her.

She glared right back, then turned to Dani, "I used to work with him at G and R Media. He left after

I did and went to Mecca, but now he's at that *struggling* rival news outlet. Remember, he's the one I told you about?" She looked back at him. "You know, the egotistical, opinionated, know-it-all." She put as much ice and disdain as she could muster into every word of her scathing description.

"Who? Me?" He shrugged, then chuckled. "Opinionated, know-it-all, was it? And that's a bad thing because…? Oh, and we're far from struggling. Got the Pulitzers to prove it. As you well know, Marly."

His voice was that same deep, cultured rumble she remembered.

And the way he said her name…

Ooo…

Smooth as silk, but with just that guttural edge to the 'A'. Like he was testing it out, to see if the taste of it was a fit…for the back of his tongue.

Dang…

It should be illegal is what it should be. That pronunciation, and with his voice. Affecting her at a near cellular level like that. Making her just want to melt. Into a puddle. At his Hermès loafers-covered feet.

She dragged her gaze back up to his eyes and forced her face to smirk at him instead.

"So…you told Dani about me, huh? What can I say…I'm just so touched you care that much." He put his right palm up to the left side of his chest, tilted his head to the side, and bowed, like a perfect gentleman. But then gave her a rakish grin.

Okay, so def not doing this…

"Actually, you know what?" She turned to Dani,

"Maybe I should take a raincheck? I forgot I've got a crazy deadline I really can't afford to miss." She spun, reached out and picked up her handbag off the entryway table where she'd just deposited it again.

"Uh yeah, I should probably be going too. You know how *cut-throat* the competition in the news business can be." She heard Insufferable saying behind her.

"Aww…come on now," Dani grasped her arm and turned her back towards her, "it's Friday night. Time to kick back and have some fun, and in as much as you're both already here, why don't you just sit and at least enjoy a good meal. Joe made his mama's famous seafood risotto; with a great twist you have just *got* to taste to believe." Dani held onto her arm as her gaze jumped back and forth between her and… Insufferable.

"Wait…Joe cooked?" His eyes and expression lit up, reminding her of just how cute she'd thought he was.

At first…

"Now, I know you didn't think I did anything tonight. You should know me well enough by now to know I am not even a little ashamed to say I can't cook to save my life!"

They all smiled at that.

"Trust me, it is no secret Joe did not marry me for my culinary skills, okay? Oh, I tried. I really did. When we were first together. Didn't I babe?"

"Don't remind me." Joe barked out a laugh as he dodged her fake punch to his arm.

"So anyway, yes…Joe cooked tonight, and I know that look you just had on your face, Dax." Dani nodded and smiled as she pointed at him. "It's the same one I used to get when Joe and I were in college, back when he only cooked for me occasionally. There I was, hanging around his apartment, conveniently at dinner time, jonesing for my next *hella*-delicious hit. Like a dang food-crack addict." She giggled and then reached out for his hand.

"Oh, I remember, babe." He grinned, used their clasped hands to pull her to him. He dropped a quick kiss on her upturned lips.

"Oh, well, say no more. I just love a good risotto. Plus, you had me at 'hella', Dani." Insufferable grinned. "There's no way I'm missing out on one of Joe's culinary masterpieces. I'm definitely staying then…especially if *Sparky* here…has decided to leave."

His tone dry, he raised his left eyebrow at her.

"What…did you just call me?" She eyed him.

"Did I stutter?" His voice dropped a couple octaves.

His smile–

Stunning.

Ooo…

Oh no, he didn't!

She took a deep breath and gritted her back teeth so hard she thought they might crack. "Well…in that case. I've changed my mind. I'm staying too." She flung her handbag back onto the table and fake smiled at him. "Dani? Can I help you guys with anything in the kitchen?"

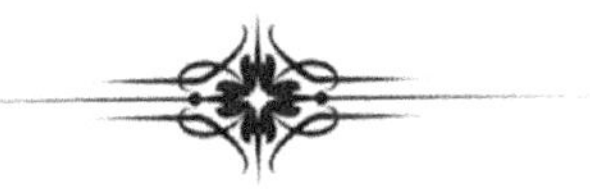

"Okay, so is it just me, or do those two remind you of us when we first met?" Alrissa wondered about the palpable tension between Marly and Dax, after they said their goodbyes and climbed into Duncan's car outside.

"Yep, worse actually." He started it up. The Mustang's engine thrummed with the rumbling sound of barely leashed power. "I give 'em about three months…four, tops, before they both can't keep their hands off each other. Oh, they'll put up a good fight, but the pheromones never lie, and the ones coming off those two were so thick, you could cut them with one of Joe's knives. Prob'ly gonna be even worse than he and Monzo are, once they get married."

He groaned.

Then he turned to look at her. The left side of his mouth twitched upward in a half smile. "Or, maybe even us..."

"Mm-hmm…only in private," she nodded.

He started to lean in, and she met him more than halfway, recognizing his intention straight off. Watched enthralled, as his blue gaze intensified beyond normal…Exploding into intriguing. Enveloping. Arousing intent. A second before they came together.

Eager, she clung to his neck and one steely bicep as he kissed her… Deep… Hot… Savage… Greedy.

Devouring her mouth over and over, like he hadn't eaten in days, and she…his very favorite delicacy.

He pulled back.

"Work's over, Gorgeous." He gave her a look.

She knew what that meant.

"Yes, it is, Detective."

He reached up, pulled the few pins out of her hair that held her updo in place and set them in the car's center console. She shook her head, letting her hair tumble down past her shoulders.

"*Oh,* baby… just how I like it," his voice ragged, he plunged his fingers in. Inhaled sharply, as he urged her head forward and set his eager lips to hers once again.

"Which reminds me…" She took in a shaky breath when he swept her hair aside and moved onto nibbling on her neck. "I know we've got…oh…that…uh…thing…early in the morning. But do we still have time tonight…mmm…that feels so-ooo good… Do you think you could come back to my place? Show me the…ooo…the…uh…next hidden treasure on our list of…um…what'd you call it? 'Not quite all the way' destinations we should visit, mmm…like you promised?"

He dragged his talented lips off her neck and reached for her left hand. Held her gaze as he placed a couple soft and sensual kisses on the backs of her fingers, right up to the exquisite engagement ring he'd placed there a couple weeks earlier. Lingered…in a way that should have been illegal.

"Absolutely," he grated, as he entwined all five of her fingers with his.

Breathless and giddy with excitement she

watched as one handed, he steered the car expertly, as they accelerated away from the driveway and made a sharp turn onto the street.

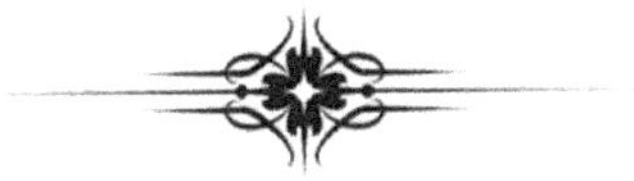

"Okay, so I'll go first. That was a straight-up train wreck." Joe groaned as he loaded up the dishwasher in the kitchen. "When you said Marly was in media and you wanted to have her over for a meal, I just immediately thought of inviting Dax. Thought they'd maybe hit it off. Go figure, they'd have a bad history, and butt heads like that."

"Yeah, I thought so too. It was my idea too, remember? Who knew, right? Still, just because they didn't have that instant connection like we did, doesn't mean they can't still get it together. Let's just give it some time." She switched on the dishwasher, patted his arm and then hopped up onto one of the nearby high stools, as a thought struck. "It just can't be a coincidence that I met them both at the International Center that day."

"Well, they are both journalists, and that was a really big story. Plus, weren't you bleeding out on the ground, one foot in heaven and one on earth, *and* only half conscious at the time?" He paused to look at her. Lifted his brows, then passed her and leaned against the side of the floating island that was the focal point of the space.

"Really, Doc?"

He grinned and shrugged.

"Actually, I met them both before I even got shot. Saw her outside on the curb as I was going in, and then Dax was just inside the Center, with the primary press group."

"Oh yeah, he called me that same morning, told me he'd seen you. Alive and kicking… his butt, was the phrase I believe he used. He said from the time you said that you were going to make yourself clear, like a shooting star, across the dark night sky, he just knew you were connected to me. Plus, from my description, he figured you just had to be my Dani. I'd told him so much about you."

"Ha! I think I remember. I didn't realize it at the time. Thought he was just being overly pushy to get his story. But he was trying to tell me he knew you, and who I was. How'd you guys even get to be friends anyway?"

"Oh, he did a piece on me, about three years ago, the first time my work got published in the New England Journal. We met for a business dinner so he could interview me, and we just hit it off from there. I can't tell you how many times I wondered if I'd shared too much with him that night. He was a virtual stranger, but as soon as he asked if I'd mind if he said a prayer over our meal, I knew he was a fellow brother in the faith. He was just so easy to talk to, and I was feeling kinda low around that time," he shrugged, "I just needed to handle some stuff I hadn't really confronted until then. I'd buried myself so deep in my work, I didn't even realize I hadn't dealt with a crisis of faith over losing you. And he really helped me see that. Prayed with me nearly every time we met in the weeks and even months following. Got me started on a path back to real healing. Couldn't believe he was only twenty-eight at the time. With every word he spoke, I could tell he was keenly intelligent and had a degree of spiritual maturity and discernment I just found astounding. He still does.

"After he called me that afternoon, I cancelled all the speaking engagements I had for the next two days, at the medical conference I was at. I couldn't get any commercial flights, so I just got on the first hover-cab I could find, paid the guy a small fortune, and flew all the way from Washington, non-stop. Don't even wanna think about how many laws we probably broke making that trip. Was headed to the Center, till Dax called back to tell me you'd been shot, and they were taking you from there to my hospital, of all places."

"Well, praise God. Your over-share saved my life Doc." She stretched over and squeezed his hand where it was resting on the island. "You were the only one who could have performed my heart surgery the way you did. If he hadn't called you, I'd be dead right now, for real." Her voice got quiet when she remembered just what kind of peril she'd been in that day.

"Think I nearly went into cardiac arrest myself, more than once, with all the monumental highs and lows of that day." He shook his head as he returned the pressure she exerted, to keep their hands clasped, and ran his other hand through his hair. "First celebrating and praising God because Dax was so sure he'd met you. Then learning you'd been wounded, very nearly fatally." He looked across at her, his eyes glazed over with moisture. "I didn't know what to think. I just kept praying and hoping that I hadn't found you, only to lose you again.

"You were so strong, the way you made it through that really complicated surgery, and I thought we were out of the woods, but then in recovery, your heart just stopped." He took a deep breath. "I was so terrified I'd done something wrong."

"No, never. You are a remarkable, world-renowned surgeon, Joseph Almonzo." She searched his beautiful eyes as she cupped a hand to the side of his face for a moment. "I think that was maybe just the time the good Lord chose to show me exactly what I needed to see, when I had my near-death experience. You know, it's like you said. I think back on it now and I really don't believe I would have been able to get back to you, whole, and healed in my spirit, were it not for that incredible encounter. It was a day of miracles for real. Starting with you, performing that *amazing* surgery."

"You mean starting with you. Speaking that completely random phrase of mine to Dax that morning. Dax remembering the connection to me and being moved enough that he just had to call me at that very moment. The exact moment before I was ready to switch off my phone to go into my next session. If all that isn't the hand of the Almighty, I sure don't know what is."

"Amen to that. Where there's a will, there's always a way. So, that's exactly why I still say I see a path for Dax and Marly to get together. I have a good feeling about those two. I really think there's some chemistry there."

"You're kidding me, right? All night I kept thinking I should prob'ly put away my pro-chef knives and any other sharp objects, and tell you to go bury your guns somewhere out on the grounds." He shook his head and gave a dry chuckle.

"Well, I didn't say it was good chemistry. I just think even that kind of negative energy sizzling between them could just as easily turn into something positive. Plus, she better get her own 'cause I would hate to have to beat a sister down, for real."

"Huh?"

"What would you say if I told you I think my young friend may have a little crush on you?" She kicked off her shoes, jumped off her stool, and slid over to where he was leaning against the island.

"Nuh-uh, no way." He snorted and gave a vigorous shake of his head as he looked down at her.

"Oh, yes way."

She grasped his hand, entwined their fingers, and gazed up into his eyes the way she'd seen Marly doing earlier that night.

He rubbed a thumb over the backs of her fingers then raised them to his lips for a couple potent kisses.

"Oh, I saw the way she looked at you. And I'll tell you what I'd say. It better stay just a crush 'cause trust and believe, friend or not, I'll show her what's up."

"Oh yeah? And what would you do, Detective?" He turned her hand over and placed an open-mouthed kiss right in the center of her palm this time.

"As you know, I own a couple of guns, Doc, and I know how to use 'em. Plus, I know people. People who know people, who are real good at chopping up and burying body parts." She flashed him a cheeky grin.

His next kiss wavered as his face fell. "Seriously?"

"Really, Joey? Are you kidding me?" She giggled, snatched her hand away and pointed up at his nose. "You should just see the look on your face, right now."

"Oh, you got me, for real. Given your profession? Don't even joke about something like that, babe."

"I can't believe you." She slapped the same hand to his chest. Felt his muscled pecs flex beneath her fingers.

"Come on now..." She ran her index finger down the center of his chest and solid abdomen, right to where the top of his slacks rode low on his hips, "You should know by now," she lowered her voice to a breathy whisper, "the only body part I'd *ever* *bury*...is yours." She looked up again and gave him a pointed look.

His beautiful eyes grew wide...

"Watch yourself, Detective. I may just have to make a citizen's arrest. Because the way you're looking at me...and what you're doing right now..."

His deep groan was like her clarion call.

"...Oh, yeah...that's def gotta be illegal in this state."

"Only this one? Then dang, I must not be doin' it right, Doc."

She popped her brows up and gave him 'the look'.

He gave her *his* look – all intense. Absorbed.

Heated. Fierce.

He growled low and feral.

She gasped, pulled away from him, and then giggled as she made a run for it into their living space. Easily dodged him as they darted around a few pieces of furniture. Then finally let him catch her as she circled back towards the kitchen, and he lunged for her. He shouted in triumph as he scooped her up from the side, swung her around, and joined their mouths in a hot, sweet duel, as with feet off the ground, she clung to his shoulders and neck.

"Playtime's over?" She pressed a few more breathy, deep kisses to his lips as she slid her fingers up from his neck, into the thick waves of his salt and pepper hair.

"Aww yeah, Detective…let's go bury *my* gun."

"Nuh-uh, you better trust and believe, this here … oh, it's all mine."

"Is that right?"

"Hell yeah… come on now, Doc. Now you know that's right."

"Aww yeah…and it's on now… got me all riled up… hope you're ready for me, babe, 'cause it's about to get buck wild up in here…"

She shrieked as he hoisted her up and over his shoulder. Kept their arousing banter going as he took the stairs up to their room…

Three at a time.

Chapter 3

Psalms 104:1&4
Bless the LORD, O my soul. O LORD my God, thou
art very great; thou art clothed with honour and
majesty. Who maketh his angels spirits; his
ministers a flaming fire…

"So, what's up this time, Svik? Gonna distract me again with another body part, so I don't ask about our fallen rivals? 'Cause, hey, you *could* let me see if those big, strong biceps of yours look even half as good as my husband's, once they're free of those hella-expensive jackets and shirts you always wear." Dani smiled and batted her eyes at Svikari over her morning cup of coffee, as he arrived at their favorite table on the curb.

"And a good Tuesday morning to you as well, Detective." He sat down opposite her as usual and unbuttoned his jacket before leaning back in his chair.

Automatically, her gaze was drawn to the section of his chest that his action revealed. To the chiseled stretch of muscled pecs, clearly visible beneath the fine fabric of his tight, thin, pristine…white shirt…

She gasped.

"Oh no, you didn't!" She barked out a laugh. "You did not just do that to me… Again! You are unbelievable, you know that?" She snorted and laughed out loud. "You're enjoying this, aren't you?"

"And I should know to what you're referring…because Detective?" His left brow rose slowly, along with the left side of his mouth, which twerked upward in a delightful half smile.

"Oh, you're good. I'll give you that," she pointed at him and continued laughing.

"Seriously, though," he leaned forward and caught her attention with his bright blue gaze. "I called you here this morning because it's time to advance our little chess game, a bit further. Another of my colleagues, who's on our side, is in play. He's working as a press liaison with Verndari, so he and Marly, together, should be able to make some waves. Start getting the word out about some of their more clandestine and unseemly activities. Once they leak some details that get people's attention, it will put a real dent in the advance of their agenda."

"Wait…Marly? How do–"

He gave her the look.

"Never mind." She pursed her lips and shook her head. "You'd think by now I'd remember you're just all up in my business, aren't yuh? Okay, so who's this new guy?"

"Remember when I told you I'm a warrior where I'm from?"

She nodded.

"Well, let's just say he's *the* leading communications specialist."

"For real?"

He nodded.

"Okay, sounds ideal for somebody to help get the word out, I guess. What do you need me to do?"

"Just like Al did, when he met with you. Just tell her to expect a friend, of a friend. He'll do the rest."

"How *is* Al, anyway? I wanted to thank him for all his great advice. It really helped me at a time when I didn't even know myself, just how much I needed it. He said he'd be around, but I haven't laid eyes on him since that day he came to the precinct."

"Oh, he's keeping busy, and don't give it another thought. I'm quite sure he knows just how much you appreciate him."

"Keeping busy?"

He nodded, once.

"What's an old guy like that busy doing? Other than playing holo-bingo at his neighborhood senior citizens' center?"

"You'd be surprised." He pierced her with his blue gaze as his left eyebrow climbed almost to his hairline.

"Uh-huh…" She tapped her fingernails on the table between them. "Knowing what I do about you now, Svik… I betcha I wouldn't."

She grinned.

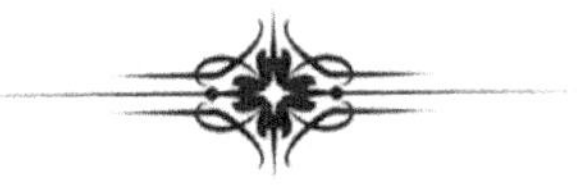

"So, what do you think, should I tell Marly what we suspect? That Verndari are the one third? The fallen angels?"

"I dunno Monzo. You didn't ask your GQ-holo guy about that part?"

"No, I didn't." She glared at him. "And his name's Svikari. *AND*…he's not *MY* anything, as you well know Duncan… Dang!"

Peeved, Dani shook her head as she took note of the tightness that always seemed to appear along his jawline whenever they talked about her possibly angelic, otherworldly colleague. "How many times do I have to say that? And what is it with you and the GQ-holo thing, anyway?"

"Long story." He scratched a finger into his dark blond mane as he shook his head.

"Uh-huh…" She tapped her fingernails on the table they were sitting at, in a private and confidential conference room of the 15th precinct.

She gasped as light dawned.

"It's Rissa, isn't it?! He was connected to that same case we were on in January with that serial-killing, rogue defender, when you met her. What'd she tell you about him, to get you all hot under the collar like that? Huh? The man is tasty." She rocked back in her chair. "And she does like 'em blond and buff. HA!"

"Really?" He shook his head again, but this time

he looked pleased, but still like he was trying to hide his smile.

"Come on now…you can tell me what she said, that's got you so riled. What's that you're always saying to me about unburdening my soul, so I'll feel better? Seems like you got some stuff you need to release yourself. Woo-sah, Detective." She roared with laughter and clapped her hands together a couple times.

"Yeah, yeah. Laugh it up while you can, Monzo, because the comedy portion of the program is now over. Moving on." He gave a dry chuckle and rotated his index finger in the air between them. "Look, I think if he didn't tell you to say anything to her about the supposed one third, then maybe you shouldn't."

"Well…remember, technically he hasn't actually acknowledged that I'm right about any of that."

"See, even more reason to keep a lid on that part of it for now. Plus, she's likely already about to be thrown into the deep end with what we *have* been able to confirm, about defenders taking hosts, and shapeshifting, and all that crap. How do you think she's gonna handle a demon-reveal type situation, on top of everything else, all at once?"

"Prob'ly not very well. Good point."

"You said you trust him, right?"

"Yeah. Without a doubt."

"Exactly. So then just trust him, and this friend of his, to tell Marly whatever she needs to know, when she needs to know it."

"Hmm…"

"What?"

"No, it's just, that's exactly what Joe told me about how he thinks God operates, when I told him about the life lesson I got from my near-death experience."

"Wise man."

"Yes, he is."

"And maybe, your…uh…maybe this…*Svikari* guy, *if* he really is an angel like you think, and if he's close to God…" He shrugged.

"The close…est…" She nodded, the words just popping out of her mouth. Just as something flashed through her mind, interrupting her train of thought.

She'd seen a moving painting once, in an art museum. Of a warring Archangel Michael, rising over and over again, high up into a dark night sky. With a sword like lightning and fire, drawn before him, and his luminescent white, thickly feathered, just massive wings, outstretched. Both, creating an arc of blinding light all around him, obliterating the retreating darkness. His face–Splendid. Flawless. Set in confident and studied, righteous determination, like he was ready to confront and utterly decimate an entire legion of evil, singlehandedly.

"Where I come from, I'm…a warrior, with responsibility for many warriors and those placed under our protection. Fighting…for a world, continually at war…"

Thanks to his reminder that very morning, his words from a few months earlier came right back to her, echoing through her mind, and resonating now with new, and startling clarity.

"What now?" Wright peered at her.

"Uh…nothing."

Smiling, she resolved to keep this, her latest little revelation, to herself for the moment.

And close to her heart.

Chapter 4

Titus 3:1
Put them in mind to be subject to principalities and powers, to obey magistrates, to be ready to every good work...

What a revelation.

Marly wiped her fingers on a napkin, folded her sandwich neatly back into its wrapper, and placed it down, onto the park bench beside her. When she'd bought her new high-tech glasses, she never expected them to revolutionize her life to the degree they had so far.

She tapped the answer button on the side of them, as she heard the incoming call alert. "Hey Dani. What's up?" The turquoise tint of the lenses flickered, and Dani's image popped up on a 2-D virtual screen projected for her eyes only by her visual tech.

"Hi Marly. How's it going?"

"I'm great! It's such a lovely early summer day out. I just decided to have lunch in the park today." She waved a hand in front of her eyes to switch the view, and then looked around, so Dani could have a glimpse of the view she had. Of people out walking in shorts and tank tops, the pretty shrubs and flowers ruffled by a gentle breeze, and the sheer beauty of everything, kissed by the golden sun.

"Wow! That looks amazing and so real. Like I could reach out and touch everything myself. You got those new, hella-expensive Televisio-tech glasses I've seen advertised, didn't you?"

Marly switched the view back and grinned. "Yep. I decided to treat myself and they are so awesome," she sang, "besides, it's only money, right?"

"That's what I'm sayin'! You go girl! And enjoy that day out for me too, for real. Because it may be winter by the time I clear my latest case load." She shook her head on a frown.

"That bad huh?"

"You have no idea. Yuh know what it is, don't you? Just too many devil-damn people out there in need of the Lord, *AND* a good shrink. I'm just sayin'." She held up her hands.

"Amen. I heard that."

"Oh, thanks again for inviting me to dinner the other night. And thank Joe for me too. Wow, he is really just such an amazing cook! Yuh know, I really think he missed his calling. He could seriously be an award-winning chef."

"Oh no, don't go there. As he was always so

quick to remind me, when we were younger, he's first and foremost the good doctor. That master chef thing is just a hobby and work stress-reliever. I used to think like you, right up until he saved my life. Trust and believe, I've never been more grateful than I am now, for the decision he made to choose the medical profession, so many years ago."

"Wow, that's amazing." Marly recalled that fateful day and knew what she was saying was true.

"Oh, and I also meant to call and apologize, just in case things got a little too awkward between me and Insufferable." She winced the minute the words were out.

"Insufferable?" Dani giggled. "Is that what you call Dax?"

"Uh-yeah, sorry. That just slipped out. I know he's a good friend to you and Joe. That was way out of line."

"He's a good guy, yuh know."

Marly opened her mouth to protest.

"Just hear me out." Dani held up a hand. "I know there's some history and obviously some bad blood there, but I really think you should reconsider your opinion of him. He's bright and fun. He's got a great job. A successful career. I'm telling you, girl; you could do a lot worse than hitching yourself to that tall drink of yummy-licious.

"Plus, you guys have so much in common. I just feel like you two could really hit it off if you'd just give him a second chance. You were both really young, and prob'ly really dumb, when you had your falling out. Where's your spirit of forgiveness, woman?"

"Today's Tuesday, right?"

Dani nodded.

"Nuts!" She snapped her fingers. "I only dust that off and bring it out every other Friday. So, what can I say? You're crap outta luck. Sor…ry." She tilted her head to the side and made a fake sad face.

Dani giggled and clapped her hands together. "Oh, you got me! Now that there was a good one. I gotta remember to use that. But come on now…seriously. Promise me you'll at least think about it?"

"Already done. I'm only kidding about the forgiveness thing. I did that a while ago as part of my faith journey. You know what they say in bible study, forgiveness isn't for the other person. It's for you."

"Preach girl. I heard that."

They touched virtual hands in a fist bump.

"Speaking of which, and most important, from what Joe tells me, and from what I've seen for myself, Dax is strong, I mean like really rock-solid in the faith. And as someone married to one of God's faithful, trust me when I tell you, there is absolutely nothing sexier, or more powerful than a man who knows how to love you 'cause he's learnt from *THE* best – the very source of true love. The bright and morning star. The Alpha and Omega. The author and finisher of our faith. Can I get an 'Amen', my sister."

"Absolutely. Amen and Amen to that, Dani. You took us to church right there." She felt her pores raise. Felt that little tingle of inspiration she always got whenever she heard, or read something that really resonated in her spirit.

"Still, I just can't *forget* what he did though, and

how terrible it made me feel at the time. I mean, I know you think he's faithful and all, but what kinda person does that?"

"Well, if yuh told me what he did, maybe I could weigh in. Feel like talking about it?"

"No. Absolutely not. I don't like the place of rage I get to whenever I let my mind go back there. Trust me, you wouldn't like me when I'm angry."

"What in the hell?!"

"What?! What is it?!" She felt her heart leap into her throat at the sudden look of terror on Dani's face as she lurched back in her chair.

"Girl, the dang AI on those new glasses of yours just turned you into the Hulk for a minute."

"Oh my gosh! My bad. Think I forgot to take off the interpretive character filter last time I used it."

"Yuh nearly gave me a heart attack Marly! And after what I've been through, with that guy almost taking me out. What's up with that? Are yuh trying to finish the job?"

"No! Never. Of course not. I'm so sorry, Dani."

"What in the hell would you even need a character filter like that for? Yuh know what… never mind. I don't even wanna know."

"It looked amazing though, didn't it?"

"Girl, you know it. Big and green and so real, I swear I almost reached for my gun. Felt like I was in the middle of an Avengers movie, or something."

They both burst into giggles.

"Look, getting back to Dax though. Whatever it is that happened between you two was in the past. Maybe he's changed, or maybe, just maybe, you were wrong about him. Did you consider that possibility? Either way, just give it some more prayerful thought at least, will you?"

"Okay, fine," she groaned.

"Oh no, Ms. Thing. I know you did not just roll your eyes at me."

Marly giggled.

"Damn, I gotta get off this line. You got me talkin' to you like I'm your mama, or something. And me in the very prime of my life. As if!" She shook her head as her laughter faded. "Okay so listen, why I called you in the first place. Remember what we talked about, given our mutual *concern* over the way things have been progressing in the world around us lately?" Even through the screen, Marly could feel the weight of her pointed gaze.

"Uh…yeah." She knew she was referring to the negative impacts of the Verndari agenda that seemed to be growing at an alarming rate. There was quite a buzz about their looming threat to humanity across the underground 'truth to power' social media sites, but somehow, they were still managing to stay under the radar as they continued to bankroll and control mainstream media, as they sanitized the content going out to the public at large.

"Well, I called you because I need you to meet with a friend of mine. Well, not exactly my friend, but he's friends with someone I know, and trust. A lot. With my life even. I think this guy I'm talking about is gonna be able to help get the word out. Maybe start a new movement of awareness and change, in a way no one's been able to before. So will you do it, will you meet with him?"

"Yeah sure, of course. You've def piqued my

curiosity. What's his name? How do I contact him?"

"No clue, but he'll reach out to you. And there's something else I should tell you. Don't be alarmed, but he's likely not going to be what you might expect, just like my friend. He's completely dissociated himself from his former work colleagues." She tilted her head to the side and eyed her through the screen. "Let's just say he may dress like them, but on the inside, where it really counts, they're nothing alike. It's something in the eyes too. You'll see, and if he's anything like my friend, trust and believe, you better buckle up 'cause girl you're in for a wild ride."

Dani's pretty face lit with such a contagious mixture of excitement and joy; Marly couldn't help but catch her enthusiasm.

"Well, okay then let the rodeo begin, I guess."

"My girl! I knew you'd be a team player. Welcome to the revolution. Okay, so call me? As soon as you know what's what?"

"Will do. Later." She waved as Dani rang off.

She tapped the side of the glasses to end the connection, then looked down and unwrapped her half-eaten sandwich so she could finish her lunch.

"Ms. Sparks?"

Her gaze snapped up.

"Uh…yeah." She put her forefinger across her lips, her words coming out garbled, around the big bite she'd just taken.

"I believe your friend Danielle told you to expect me? You can call me Budbringer." He executed a neat little bow.

"And I…am at your service."

Chapter 5

Proverbs 2:10
When wisdom entereth into thine heart, and
knowledge is pleasant unto thy soul…

Marly drew in a breath too quickly and all but choked on her bite of sandwich.

Coughing, she reached out for her cup of soda pop. Used the time it took to pull up a fair amount of it through the straw, so she could take *him* in, full measure.

Well, hullo Chris Pine's, charismatic Captain Kirk…meets Alan Ritchson's, rugged Reacher…meets her very favorite 'late forties-ish, hot guy with a foreign accent' fantasy.

Only, taller more muscled…and way hunkier…

Oh, my…

Verndari sure made 'em big, didn't they?

And what's that he said? He was at her service? His deep velvet tone and British accent resonated with her at a nearly visceral level. Appealing to and feeding her historical romance-reading soul, she supposed.

Dani was right…this was already shaping up to be quite a ride…let the rodeo begin, indeed.

He smiled wide, turning his face into just this absolutely gorgeous canvas of untold possibilities. While his stunning blue eyes seemed to look right into her, piercing and then imprinting his very essence on her soul.

"Do you mind if I sit?"

"Oh…uh…no, of course, please." She pulled herself up a bit and shifted to her left, as he turned and sat with manly grace. His muscled thighs set so wide apart that when he turned towards her, his left knee almost touched her. Almost.

"So, from what I've been hearing from Verndari, there's a continuing and concerted effort afoot, to distort and quash the truth about their, shall we say, self-serving, and just downright distasteful behavior, and activities. The war is raging on, Ms. Sparks. The war for men's minds. And information is key. The more you know, the better to make an informed decision. I, and others like me who stand apart from them, have infiltrated their ranks. I've been set up as a press liaison between them and the human population. So, unbeknown to them, I'm well poised to turn the tables on those soulless pretenders, and to help usher in a new, enlightened chapter in earth's history.

"What say you and I put our heads together, and see if we can't start by creating a rather large wrinkle in their Godforsaken agenda, shall we?"

She listened, absorbed, then decided on her first query.

"Um, I'm curious. How exactly did you find me just now? And so quickly?" She peered at him. "I literally just got off the line with Dani, no more than a minute before you popped up, right in front of me?"

"Ah, bright girl, cutting right to the chase then, are we? I like that." He beamed at her. "What would you say if I told you, that from the outset, you should simply assume that if I need to, I can find you, anywhere, at any time?"

"I'd say, you sound like a serial killer...or a stalker. At best. So, you should know, I've got cans of mace and pepper spray in my purse, *and* Dani, my really good friend, is in the NYPD. Oh, and FYI, she's a crack shot with her gun. How 'bout them apples?"

He threw back his head and roared with laughter.

"You've got *two* tins in there?" He pointed to her pocketbook.

She nodded and pulled it in a bit closer to her side of the park bench.

"Really?"

She nodded again.

"Oh, I like you already, Ms. Sparks. You and I, I can tell. We are going to get along just famously, without a doubt."

He hadn't exactly explained how he'd done what he did, but she couldn't help herself; she smiled right back. Even giggled, carried along as she was by his contagious, obvious, and inherent joy for life.

Dani said she trusted her friend with her life, and if he was anything like this guy, she could see why. He was a stranger to her, and a defender to boot, but something about sitting there and laughing with him like they were old friends just clicked. Instantaneous and meaningful. Like meeting a kindred soul in the most unlikely of places and circumstances.

"So, I haven't decided if I can actually trust you yet, but if I did, tell me, where would we even start?"

"Why, at the beginning of course." He quit smiling. His shrewd gaze brought her right back to the moment. "Where the police and every good reporter finds and begins to pursue the most critical evidence."

He paused and eyed her.

"The scene of the crime?" He gestured with a hand.

The expression on his face became one of expectancy, and finally, it dawned on her.

"Oh, of course. You're talking about the supposed alien crafts they arrived in that just disappeared, never to be seen again."

He nodded.

"I always wondered about that. From everything I read, none of the news agencies at the time, not even the big mainstream media outlets were ever able to get a straight answer from them regarding how that was even possible. They all just gave up and stopped asking questions eventually."

"That's right."

Her mind swarmed with a host of ways she could

revive the very old story. "I can start that buzz going again. Remind my readers of the gaps in their recollection. Everything that points to defenders not exactly being the forthcoming and trustworthy saviors of mankind they pretend to be.

"That's such a great lead! Thanks so much for that. I'll get right on it and see what else I can resurrect to stir up the dirt that's gonna eventually bury them. You know, I got promoted after a story I wrote just a little while ago on the bomb threat at the International Center, and the near fatal shooting of a leading NYPD detective. My friend I mentioned, by the way."

He nodded. "Well, good for you! I'm sure that promotion was very well deserved."

She beamed. "I've been angling ever since for a really big story that could push my career forward to the next level. I think this could be it."

She felt a fire rise in her, and barely noted the deficit, when she looked to him for an answering energy. He appeared concerned, hesitant even.

Thinking of the time, she consulted her watch. "Well, sorry to cut this short, but my lunch hour is almost over, and I've got to get back. It's been…ah…interesting?" She smiled and extended her hand.

"Indeed." He shook it and returned her smile.

She shouldered her handbag and started to get up from the bench.

"Just a word of advice, if I may." He placed a gentle hand on her arm, halting her rise. "I don't think I need to remind you of the delicacy of an operation such as this. It demands a bit of discretion, and diplomacy, obviously. Give no thought to me, but I am concerned for you… After all, we wouldn't want to attract unwanted and dangerous Verndari scrutiny. Or, put off your viewership before you've even got them on the hook."

"Oh, of course, say no more." She nodded, beginning to rise again.

"Or…" he touched her arm again, "incur a lawsuit, that could potentially see you dismissed? Hmm?"

That one gave her pause.

"Really?"

"Verndari control the wealth of over half of the planet. They exert tremendous influence with certain global players and high-ranking government officials, both foreign and domestic, right here in the US. Make no mistake, they are the gate keepers, holding all the keys, and wielding what they believe to be unstoppable power."

Marly felt the impact of his words like an ice bath in the arctic. Here she was ready to go off all gung-ho and eager to chase down a story, and enlighten the public, with little thought for the very real and potentially dangerous consequences.

"Chin up, Ms. Sparks, have no fear. That's precisely why I'm here. To provide guidance and structure. What's that American expression of yours. We've got this?"

She nodded, feeling better.

"Okay, so rather than involving your media house right off the bat, I suggest we start relatively small, with your underground presence. With what is it? Just over fifty thousand followers?" She nodded, impressed that he'd obviously done his research on her, while at the same time just the tiniest bit alarmed that he had so thoroughly infiltrated her digital life.

Lots of people had created avatars and joined the underground since the defenders first made their appearance. Unlike the dark web, which was a haven for illegal and nefarious activities, the underground was its antithesis – a hub of 'truth to power' and conscious voices, standing up to corrupt systems of government, and every kind of social injustice, and all endeavoring to bring awareness, and make the world a better place for humankind.

"So do I want to know how you know so much about me and my social media presence in the underground?"

"Doubtful, but suffice it to say, I'm well versed in what I do. Something that I trust in time you will come to appreciate. Even rely on."

He said it with no hint of pride or artifice. For him, she could see, it was merely a simple statement of fact.

And she believed him.

He looked down and touched his watch a couple times.

"I took the liberty of creating a new and separate profile for you, still linked to all your followers on those platforms, but that no one can trace back to you. It will be an ideal vehicle for you to begin to 'stir up the dirt' as you put it, but without it coming back to haunt you."

He touched his screen again and she got an immediate alert popping up in the right lens of her glasses.

"There. And all my contact info is included as well, so feel free to reach out at any time. I'll be pleased to be a sounding board for you. You know, maybe vet your initial communications before you post them?"

"Thank you, I believe I'd appreciate that."

"Brilliant. Right. Off you go, then. Oh, and stay safe and blessed, my intrepid reporter." He touched his fingers to an imaginary brim of a hat and nodded with a charming smile.

"Intrepid?" She looked down at her feet for a moment before meeting his eyes again. "There's nothing fearless about me." She shook her head.

"That's because you don't yet see what I do. Speak those things which be not as though they were, Ms. Sparks, and trust me, they *will* come."

And there it was again. That little tingle of inspiration. Uplifting her spirit and resonating with her as deeply as the wisdom shining out of the depths of his piercing blue gaze.

"Yuh know, you said to call you Budbringer, but if it's all the same to you, I think I'll shorten that." She smiled, loving his farewell words.

All of them.

"You stay blessed as well, *Buddy*." She turned and walked quickly away, towards a garbage receptacle to deposit her trash.

He cocked his head to the side, "Not sure that's

a keeper, but I suppose it will grow on me."

"It better. Because I'll be personally making sure that everyone, including the big guy, calls you that for the next earth millennium, at least."

"Really, Alcindor?"

Alrissa Cole's guardian popped in, with a broad grin on his face, and visible to just him, as they watched Marly move further away with her guardian close at her side.

"You know, you could learn a thing or two from Verge." He jerked his chin up in the direction of the guardian's receding back. "Shouldn't you be looking out for Alrissa right about now?"

"Oh, she's fine, just having a little personal time with Duncan at the moment."

"Ah," he nodded. "So how are you coping? Getting those parental-parallel, withdrawal symptoms yet?"

"Some. It's strange, being with her every second when she was a child, a baby, and even before, from the very instant she was conceived. Then watching her grow up, and now, realizing she may need me less and less…in the time she has left, before she comes home." He got a wistful look on his face. "I've done this so many times before, with so many others. But each and every time, it's still such an adjustment, for sure."

"Well, you better get ready brother because they'll be tying the knot soon, and if you think you're hardly seeing her now, just wait until you start experiencing those odd little Father and Creator inspired separation, sad feelings. Because with those two, after their wedding day, you'll be lucky if you see her at all, after that first time, and once they really start–"

"AH-AH-AH! Moving on." Al's face contorted as he rotated his forefinger in the air.

Gabriel had a chuckle, then got back to the negotiation at hand.

"Okay, so how about a quarter millennium? Have a heart Al. It's a popular name for our furry friends, after all."

"Please, you could do a quarter in your sleep. Well, if we ever slept. Three quarters at least, I think."

"A half?"

"Deal." Al bumped fists with him and grinned. "Oh, and cheers, old chap. Chuffed to bits we had this little chat. Toodle-oo, and so on, and so forth."

"Really?"

Al disappeared with a roar of laughter.

He shook his head, then grinned.

Inhaling a focused breath, he took a moment to get recentered in the perfect will of the Creator.

Ever ready to be of service, he tuned into the hum of internal voices around him.

Chapter 6

Psalms 91:11
For He shall give His angels charge over thee, to
keep thee in all thy ways…

Marly could hear the dull hum of muffled voices around her.

But couldn't make out what they were saying over the droning sound of… What was that?

She opened her eyes and immediately wished she hadn't.

She was sitting in an underground train. Surrounded. An unwilling participant in her very worst nightmare, as more than a dozen desperate faces pressed in on her, all at the same time.

Mouths moving but emitting nothing but silence, or garbled noise. Still, they tried desperately to get their messages across. Never accepting that no matter what she did, or how hard she tried to focus on the painful sounds they made, or even the articulation of their lips, she just couldn't understand them.

And even worse, she knew what came next. For soon after the futile attempts to communicate came the unpleasant grasping of clammy hands driven by frustration. Followed swiftly by the angry, frenzied, hateful attack.

Not waiting, as she felt the very first cold touch of icy fingers, she knew not from which of them, she jumped to her feet and flew. Straight through their pressing, gelatinous bodies. Out the closed window on the opposite side of the train, and up into the darkness of the surrounding tunnel. Terrified, as it began to swallow her, she closed her eyes, drew on a burst of speed, and pushed ever and ever upward. On and on through the never-ending levels of such tangible, encroaching despair.

Hoping to see just that little blessed sliver of light beneath her closed lids that would signal the end of this latest episode, and her near immediate release, she pushed onward. No matter where she found herself, she'd learned early on, the light was never ever far away. She only had to endure, until she could reach it.

She'd opened her eyes to the resident horrors, more than once before. Some aspects were thrilling at first. That remarkable, unparalleled view and sensation of passing through layers of wall, or glass, and up through ceiling, and then floor. So strange the feeling of being able to literally stomp her feet, feel them connect with a solid surface in one instant. But then float right through it, completely and utterly weightless, in the next.

She'd been fascinated by other things as well. Marveled at the sheer number and variety of inhabitants, some perfectly normal looking, while others, not so much. With the ever-changing faces and bodies constantly morphing into odd looking forms, evil-faced pretend children, mythical creatures, and even inanimate objects. There were even some that looked like 20th and 21st century sci-fi inspired humanoid life, or perhaps she had it wrong. Maybe it was those centuries' creature designers who had received *their* inspiration from the void to generate some of the ugliest, and most horrific cinematic characters ever conceived. Who knew?

Whatever the case, all were so busy. Busy moving up and down and along the maze of rooms, but still essentially doing nothing of consequence, at least as far as she could tell.

Unbelievable, really.

She'd seen everything from entire city blocks with buildings, streets and vehicles, to blistering miles of desert sand, and even dark, turbulent oceans. Mere illusion though, she learned at cost. Capable of moving you to untold heights of exhilaration in one moment, while quickly and unceremoniously snatching it all away, in the very next.

She recalled driving a car for a very short distance once. Her favorite fantasy convertible. It was a gorgeous day out. She reveled in the feel of the sun on her cheeks, the wind in her hair, and the admiring looks of pedestrians as she cruised past them. She'd closed her eyes on a smile for but a second, and reopened them to find that the car, along with the busy street she was on, all of it, vanished. Leaving her suspended, in a seated position in midair, with her hands no longer grasping a steering wheel, but holding onto exactly nothing. And in sudden, and very disorienting darkness.

Yes, she'd seen some incredible things for sure. And all somehow crammed into each of those rooms. A few about the size of her high school cafeteria. But most, considerably smaller.

All hope abandon, ye who enter here!

For real.

She'd seen that quote from Dante's *The Divine Comedy* scrawled everywhere, all over the walls and ceilings of a space she'd floated into once, barely bigger than a broom closet. Dante may have been right about the major sins that brought a soul to this tragic end, but he was for sure wrong about the number of levels of damnation to which they'd be forever condemned. For there were far more than nine.

Instead, in her experience, they were infinite.

And from such, there was neither reprieve, nor escape.

Thank God, that unlike them, she'd found she could come and go from the void just as she pleased, to appease her earlier morbid fascination, for the most part.

And at first.

Until soon enough, she'd grown to regret her initial curiosity, or perhaps it was stupidity. Either way, she'd received a rude awakening one night. The night the attacks began. She didn't even know why.

Maybe she'd been invisible before or hidden somehow. She'd stood in front of mirrors in those rooms, a couple of times, alarmed she was unable to recognize the face and body reflected there.

Or perhaps she *was* invisible, and the reflection in the mirror not hers at all.

But instead, just another kind of hellish prison, reserved for those who'd lived a life only for themselves, in self-absorbed vanity.

Where, within the frigid confines of the glass, some poor soul was forever trapped.

Or outside of it. Perpetually standing in that same spot, in the center of the room, invisible to her. To everyone. Except for that solitary, tragic reflection.

Whatever the case, at some stage, they knew that she was somehow different, not one of them.

So now, and from as soon as she learned she had the capacity, she flew. As far and as fast as she possibly could.

Just like tonight.

She could feel their sadness, depression, and regret, like a living presence surrounding her, enfolding her, restricting her breathing and beginning to pull her down. She stretched up with her right hand. Perhaps in entreaty, or in sheer desperation, and someone grasped it, in a warm firm grip. Pulled her upward, at an even faster rate than she'd ever been capable of on her own.

Almost immediately she felt the lightness of her body, no longer weighed down by the oppressive hopelessness of the lost. Up and up, they climbed, until she could feel the gentle kiss of a soft breeze against her face and ruffling the strands of her hair. She sighed in relief, opened her eyes, ready to embrace the light. But to her shock, it was still pitch black. All-encompassing and impenetrable.

Feeling a return of her earlier anxiety, she gripped her rescuer's hand even tighter.

"It's okay, you'll be fine. The light that takes you back will be here soon."

It was her angel.

With the familiar sound of rushing waters, his voice reverberated around her head, just as she remembered. She hadn't seen, or heard him, not since that first time he'd pulled her through that window, and up into a welcoming sky. She nearly sobbed in relief.

She felt his hand start to pull away.

"No, don't leave me, yet. Please?" She maintained her grip.

Drawn to him, she reached up with her left hand, ran her fingers over his thumb, and across their joined hands to his wrist. Feeling her way along the length of his arm, she floated up, until she could place her palm on his strong shoulder.

"Will you dance with me again?"

"Again?"

She felt his smile in the utterance of the single word. Could see his flawless amused face in her mind's eye, just as it had been on that fateful morning.

"Please? I know it was probably supposed to be a once in a lifetime deal, but since we're here. Just until the light comes?"

She knew she was likely asking too much. That

dance they'd shared over a year ago had served its purpose. Changing the trajectory of her life. Giving her a renewed purpose, and a boldness in faith and in her life in general she'd never displayed. But she couldn't forget it, the sheer joy of the experience. Couldn't pass up a golden opportunity to feel that bliss again, if only for a few moments.

She closed her eyes.

Held her breath.

Released it on a sigh and a smile, as she felt the palm of his hand, such a gentle touch, coming to rest at the very center of her back, just below her shoulder blades. Slowly at first, he turned her in the darkness, leading her in an ever-widening circle, and with greater energy as their joy blossomed. The wind again joined in on their fun, swirling around them as they twirled, in blissful silence.

A spark of light flared and grew behind her closed eyelids.

She leaned in, rested her head on his chest, felt the solid strength there. The powerful vibration of his tremendous wings traveled through his body to hers. She felt the beating of his heart, as she inhaled one last breath.

And then blew it out, as she opened her eyes.

Looked around at the familiar items in her room.

Smiling, she gave thanks as always, for the countless possibilities of the new day ahead.

And for her incomparable and most precious guardian angel.

Chapter 7

Job 8:7
Though thy beginning was small, yet thy latter end should greatly increase…

Ah, the dawning of a new day of countless possibilities…

It took a couple long nights of research, but it was finally ready.

Her inaugural post.

The opening salvo, of what she hoped would be the first of many shots across the Verndari's bow.

She'd brought Dani up to speed on her initial meeting with Buddy and how they'd decided she should do some undercover blogging as a start. Plus, she'd run this first post by him already too, and other than a few recommendations for adjusting her initial tone and subtext from accusing to questioning, she thought he was pleased. His input had also proven to be invaluable to her coming up with her sobriquet, so that was certainly an added bonus. Once she'd made those little changes, it became so clear to her what she should call herself. Dani loved her choice too. What was that phrase she'd heard her use? Oh yeah, it was clear, just like a shooting star, across the dark night sky.

Satisfied she hit the send button on her air screen and rocked back into her chair as she watched it update across several underground websites to which she was linked.

My fellow skeptical Americans…

Let's take a trip back…to when a loaf of bread was 6 bucks. You could still fit into your skinny jeans. And having a sky-medic get to the scene of an emergency in half the time of a road-bound ambulance was just a cherished dream. A very lucrative dream, in the mind of the brilliant and now uber-rich guy who invented them.

I'm talking about New Year's Day - Jan 1st, 2100. The day what it meant to be a member of our precious human race changed. Dramatically. And in all likelihood, forever.

Genderism. Gone.

Racism. Gone.

Religious, ethnic, classist, and all other discriminatory demarcations that used to divide us, just a distant memory. From the very minute the physical and sociological dynamic changed for what we define as Us, vs Them.

Great! Every country on the planet

banded together for months, like never before. Thought we'd be, all of us, engaged in the fight of our very lives.

Well...until we weren't.

Instead of being subjected to flesh melting laser beams, or 'beam me up, Scotty'. Instead of weapons of mass destruction, and alien abduction. The people of earth were met with a species who claimed they came in peace. Remarkably, mirroring every heart-warming, uplifting, feel-good, Elliot meets and befriends E.T., Sci-Fi movie ever produced.

But tell me, were you, like so many of us, urged to stop questioning how they got here in the first place? To ignore the fact that the thousands of spacecrafts that flew into our atmosphere, littering the sky on that fateful night, delivered up their occupants and then just up and vanished. POOF! Like puffs of smoke in a stiff breeze.

Stealth tech, you say? No. Because not even the most sophisticated cloaking mechanisms generated by the defenders to date can also eradicate an energy signature. Hundreds of the world's top scientists investigated, tirelessly, and found not even the minutest trace of anything. A disappearing act worthy of Houdini, the famed magician, no doubt.

So, tell me, where do you think all those ships are now?

Do you know?

Does anybody?

Dozens of reporters. The brave ones. And in the minority. They continued to try to get answers early on, and still persisted later, but were met with deflection and rejection. Many were the subject of political attacks and even unfortunate and random accidents. Some of them fatal.

Coincidence?

Can we really be expected to trust the perpetrators of what may well turn out to be the most diabolical hoax in all of earth's history?

And what of their complicit supporters in high office?

What exactly IS what I'll from now on be referring to, in this space, as 'The Defender Agenda?'

And are they really the saviors of humanity they purport to be?

You know, Plato said, "Justice in the life and conduct of the State is possible only as first it resides in the souls of the citizens."

So, at your very core, are you on the side of truth, common decency, order, and justice? Or are you content to just watch it go on, when faced with the inevitability of chaos? For make no mistake, in this pivotal moment in earth's history, chaos is not merely a possibility.

It is an absolute certainty.

So, will we speak out? Make our collective voices heard? Or, will we be silent?

You decide.

Till next time, anxious to hear from you.

Cynical in NYC

She read it over one more time, then yawned as she opened the article she was writing for her news agency. It was on the amazing new holo-park opening she'd attended over the prior weekend. In addition to being treated to all the incredibly realistic sights and sounds, each participant was afforded an opportunity to book a ten-minute sound stage to make their own reel with the park's attractions. Needless to say, the Jurassic Zone was booked solid for the entire year. Just filled with people looking to be the next big thing. The deadline for her to submit her piece was looming, and as tired as she was, she needed to get it done.

DING.

An alert came up on her air screen.

Already?

Anxious to see what kind of a response she received, and so soon, she switched back over to her social media screen and hit the open message prompt.

> *For this, what you need is - A Hot Lay 24/7.*

"Huh?" She peered at her screen.

Like her, the writer just had a generic cartoon guy avatar, to her girl. But with a comment like that, of course she already knew it just had to be a man. She zeroed in on the creep's username. She didn't recognize it.

"Digital Dante? What the hell kinda name is that? Oh, I got your 'hot lay', yuh chauvinist freak."

Peeved, she started typing a response in private chat mode…

Excuse you? So, a woman with a dissenting opinion who bravely questions the status quo should have a diversion instead? And 'needs a man' to provide said distraction? Is that it? Oh & let me guess, is this the part where you offer your stud services? Well, thanks, but no thanks. I'll pass. 😌

Tapping her fingernails on her desk she waited.

'A Hot Lay 24/7' is a handle. For THE leading 'truth to power' guy. He was there, that first night. Got some incredible footage & stories from bystanders. Just meant you should check out his posts and reels. That's all.

BTW if you really were 'brave', you'd be posting on mainstream media. Not on the underground, hiding behind some fake name.
Ms. Cynic? *Is it?* 🙄

"What?" She peered at her screen. "Who the hell *is* this guy? You do not know who you're messing with right now, buddy." Grrr…she felt her blood pressure rise as she started typing her reply.

Well, you're one to talk, Mr. Digital Dante. *Like how original. You know nothing about me. And prob'ly even less about him. Prob'ly picked that name just because of the aliteration.*

BTW in case you don't know about that word either, in literature, that's when the same letter is used at the beginning of two connected words, yuh know like Digital Dummy.

Well thanks for the English lesson, Ms. Zbornak. And FYI, alliteration is spelt with 2 Ls. Not one.

She huffed, as much from his little snippy comeback about her spelling, as from his reference to Dorothy Zbornak from one of her very favorite 20th century iconic sit-coms – '*The Golden Girls*'.

"So what? Is that supposed to be some kind of crack about age? So, first I'm a coward for posting on the underground, and now I'm old? Is that it? Ooo, the grape nuts on this guy."

She waited as he continued typing.

And, as it happens, I chose that handle deliberately. Dante is one of my favorite writers. I appreciate his POV. The way he was such a really present, in the moment observer. A perceptive critic of the political and social scene of his day – commenting on the foibles of both the rulers and the ecclesiastical hierarchies.

Well, good for you! Real impressive. Did you google that all by yourself just now, or did you phone a friend?

Was prepared to give you the benefit of the doubt but starting to see why you're unattached and don't think you, 'need a man', as you put it.

"Huh?" She sat back in her chair for a moment, digesting his words. Well, that was weird as hell. "Where'd that come from?"

Unattached?? Not that it's any of your business. Plus, it's not like I care, or anything, but how would you know?

It's after 11pm on a Friday night. Only two choices. You're either unattached or unhappily attached. I just figured the former.

Plus, the single, bright, and

proud of it, independent woman hostility of your first text nearly leapt off my screen to bug-with-an-itch-slap me in the head. 😆 *Good thing I don't have on my VR gear right now. That one woulda hurt, for real.*

She barked out a laugh, then giggled as she texted back.

Did you seriously just say bug-with-an-itch? 🤭

And what about you? You're online at this hour, same as me. What's your excuse?

I'm...particular.

Remember to check out that truther's posts & reels.

*And BTW... if I **were** to offer you my stud services, you wouldn't need to guess. You'd know. Cause it'll be because YOU asked me... Nicely. Till next time. Gnite, Ms. Cynic.*

She gasped.

Felt a tingle along her spine she hadn't expected just then, or experienced, in a very, very long time.

Not since...

She shook her head to evict the unwanted

squatter, living rent free for far too long in that primo real estate behind her feathered bangs.

"Till next time, Dante," she breathed, intrigued and disappointed he hadn't stayed online longer so they could talk some more.

Well, one thing was certain at least, her viewership was already up, by one.

And what a one…

She grinned, switched screens, and went back to finishing her article.

Chapter 8

John 8:32
And ye shall know the truth, and the truth shall
make you free…

Waiting on their usual park bench for Buddy a couple weeks later, she checked her underground profile for the latest feedback to her last post. Her viewership was way up, over a hundred thousand. Far more of an increase than she'd ever thought possible in such a short space of time.

Pleased, she started flipping through the dozens of recent comments for anything useful.

"Okay, let's see what we've got today… *Food for thought… You go girl…* Oh, hell no…" She flicked a finger in front of her glasses to scroll quickly past a response that had nothing to do with her posts. "Stalker much? Geez… moving on…*Viva la revolution…* and–" she felt a pleasant tingle creep

up her spine as she saw the next username pop up–
Digital Dante

She hesitated for a second, then tapped on the side of her glasses.

Hey, thought your last post was super insightful and thought provoking. I shared it with my followers so the word's def getting out there. Looking forward to the next one.

BTW I re-read this Dante quote the other day and immediately thought of you —

"Many have justice in their hearts, but slowly it is let fly, for it comes not without council to the bow."

Just means that sometimes plans turn out better with the joint wisdom and guidance of others. None of us have all the answers, right? So, I figured…if you're really gonna do this 'Lady Justice' thing, just want you to know you can use me. Aside from my followers, I've got some sources with interesting perspectives and theories on the reason for The Defender Agenda. It'll be my honor to help you with your righteous cause.

Till next time, Ms. Cynic.

"Oh, now isn't that interesting." She grinned, tapped her glasses to accept vocal, facial and physical cues, "Voice to text and key facial expressions and body language to emojis," and started dictating.

Use you? Really? 

Thought you were a gentleman who doesn't offer your services unless expressly asked.

She read it over and nodded so the AI would know she wanted it sent.

And not more than ten seconds later–

•••

"Okay, and he's online. Right this very minute." She felt that little tingle along her limbs increase and shook her head so the AI wouldn't type what she'd just said. She sat up straighter on the bench and peered ahead as she awaited his response.

•••

Well, that all depends on what I'm being used for, doesn't it? And if memory serves, you're the one who referenced 'stud services' that first night, not me. Plus this is different. This is serious. Like '21st century Area 51' serious.

Yeah, for real, right? As it happens, I've got some insider guidance, but the more the merrier. I'll def take you up on your offer of help to fight the power. Thks!

•••

Sure, I'll start sending anything useful your way. But 'insider guidance?' Well, that wasn't cryptic at all. 😄 *Care to elaborate?*

Absolutely not. Us incognito cynics never reveal our sources, plus you didn't hear that from me. 🙊

Ah, of course. Have no fear, your secret's safe with me.

So, you said this was different. Does that mean you don't take your stud services seriously?

Why? You interested already? 😊

Oh please. 🙄 *I'm not that desperate.*

Oh, how she doth wound me. (guy fake-stabbing himself in the heart GIF)

Ah, so you're a fan of Shakespeare, as well as Dante? Well, I take it back then. Any guy who can quote the ultra-classics is OK in my books.

And BTW I'm a 'historical

romance reading, bring me chocolates and flowers, and take me out to dinner like it's Valentine's Day, for like forev-errr,' 😬 *kinda decent, Christian girl. So, all jokes aside, don't think that fits in with the stud services theme.*

Wondering how he'd react… She held her breath–

And you deserve all of that and so much more.

–Then released it on a slow puff, as she felt the ice around her heart melt, just a little.

Plus, stud services come in all varieties. The key is to wait to be asked, just like I said. And then aim to please. Whatever the request.

Aww…a true gentleman. 😊

Not necessarily.

I'll wait for you to ask…but something tells me you won't want me to be a gentleman once you do. (Hot guy growling on a grin GIF)

Till next time, Ms. Cynic.

She put one of her index finger's knuckles to her mouth to stifle her giggles.

"Well, good morning to you Ms. Sparks. Am I interrupting?"

She spun to her right and tapped her glasses to end the link to her feed.

"Buddy…uh…no, good morning, to you too. I didn't even see you come over."

He'd managed to walk up and sit down just a few inches away from her, and she hadn't even noticed. Had she been that engrossed in her little tête-à-tête with Dante or was he doing his 'pop up and find you anywhere at any time' thing again.

How does he even do that?

"How long were you sitting there?"

"Not long."

She thought his answer imprecise, but then that was so often a part of his unique charm. What was that quirky term she'd heard Dani use? Vague-a-lisciousness? Yep, he had that in spades, for real.

"Okay, so what have you got for me today?" She tapped her glasses, "Voice to notes," and got ready to record the latest dish. "Anything juicy happening at Verndari Diplomatic Center you can share? There was some buzz around Senator Sapien's visit a couple months ago, you know the representative from New Atlantis? But he's not talking. Couldn't even score an interview with him."

"Actually, I was rather hoping to hear a bit more about you today."

"Me?"

He nodded. "During our first meeting you let on that you don't really consider yourself to be a fearless person, so were I to ask, tell me, would you say you're not particularly outgoing either?"

"Well," she tapped her glasses to switch off the AI. "I'm pretty comfortable meeting new people, if that's what you mean. Especially since that's essentially the job. But can't say I enjoy the aspects of it that sometimes make me have to go into potentially dangerous situations. Hell, I keep my own apartment like Fort Knox." She snorted

"Hmm… I thought as much. I hope you don't mind me saying, but from our interaction thus far, you seem guarded, even timid. Not exactly the kind of traits that make for an exceptional, award-winning reporter, who always gets her story. It occurs to me that I can perhaps assist with that. I've found that being a successful journalist, a success at anything really, starts with being grounded and centered in oneself. That way you can then handle whatever gets thrown at you, with confidence, and give of your best. Would you agree?"

"Uh… I suppose."

"You also seem just a tad distracted of late. So, tell me, how are you, really?"

He gave her that look. The now familiar one, where she felt his blue eyes penetrating right into her soul. Who's to say? Maybe an objective male perspective was just what she needed. So, before she could even think better of it, she took a quick breath and launched right in.

"Honestly? I'm not so sure. I'm prob'ly a walking cliché for man trouble," she gave a dry laugh, "but I'm just completely confused right now. There's this guy I know, Dax Newton. I met him about four years ago, at my first press agency. I left soon after and since then, I only saw him at media briefings, or when there was a really big story to cover. Well, at least until about three weeks ago. He made the move over to Earth Network News a while ago I heard. It's only about a block away from where I work, and now, it seems like he just keeps popping up. In my favorite café. At restaurants too. Plus, he's best buds with my really good friend's husband, so every time I go over to their house. There he is again. Annoying as ever. But still so charming though, and funny, and good-looking, and *so smart*." She shook her head and groaned. "I dunno, it's just all messed up. Then my friend? She wants me to give him another chance, see? But how can I, after what he did? I was humiliated." She felt the range of messy emotions from that awful day rise, but she pushed them down, refusing to allow them to rule her again.

"But still, I keep thinking, it just can't be a coincidence that we keep meeting up and bumping heads, right? We spent just over three phenomenal weeks together, working on one of the most significant stories of my career. I've never felt that way before, about anyone. Or since. I really thought he was the one, yuh know? I mean it was intense, and it's so strange because we never even kissed. But still, I felt this immediate and just such a powerful connection and attraction. Now, don't get me wrong, nobody loves a good romance novel more than me, but I always thought all that crap about soul mates was a bit much. But now… I don't know, maybe…

But no. That couldn't possibly be. He's not soulmate material. Right? I mean, come on…"

She glanced at him, looked again and winced, as she caught sight of his amused expression. "Oh no…did I overshare. You are seriously easy to talk to by the way. But maybe this is a bad idea. Besides, I really doubt you could help me anyway. I probably need one of those on-line relationship gurus everybody's using now."

"Oh, I think if we chat, you'll find I know a bit about what you're saying. You could even say I'm something of a messenger of love where I come from." He beamed and nodded when she raised her brows in query.

"Wow, that's so interesting. What's it like there? Your home I mean. The defenders haven't really shared anything in all the time you guys have been here."

"It's beyond anything you could ever imagine. Defies human description, really."

"Hmm… must be something to see."

"Indeed. You have no idea."

"So, a messenger of love, huh?" She eyed him.

He nodded, "And any of your earthly relationship experts are going to tell you exactly what I will. That the key to human connection…successful human connection, is in how you communicate with love. With God. As well as with your fellow man."

"Wait, God? Verndari believe in God?"

"Absolutely."

"I mean, I thought what you said that first day about calling things as though they are biblical, but it's wisdom that's been touted by secular sources too.

I just figured you got it from one of those. But you guys are believers? That's so amazing…and incredible."

"Why? Those of us who are fighting for mankind, and even those with the agenda against you, all know He exists, and who He is. God is God of every corner of the vast universe, Ms. Sparks."

"Yes. He is, isn't he?" She smiled, heartened by his declaration.

"So come on, if for no other reason, why not humor me? Go ahead, ask me anything." He turned towards her with a childlike eagerness.

"Okay, in your experience, if you had to say, what's the key, the single most critical component to the human dynamic?"

"There are three keys, actually. Basic godly values. Every time you engage someone, ask yourself, is it necessary – something that needs to be said, are you being truthful – honest with yourself and them, and is it kind. And associated with that last one, is what I call the catch-all, general rule of thumb. You can do anything, everything that makes you happy, as long as it won't hurt you, or someone else."

"Wait…isn't that true, necessary, and kind test a Buddhist, rather than a Christian thing?"

"Your history records that it has been attributed to Buddha, Ghandi, and others, but actually, I think Socrates said it first."

He eyed her as he shook his head. A look of sadness crossed his face.

"Oh, humanity, and your affinity for meaningless demarcations. When will you finally accept that there are no distinctions, no separations of any kind, in the perfect will and love of the Creator, for his flock. One day all of humanity will know that real, true love–genuine, lasting, unconditional, powerful, undeniable love, is found only in the fullness of relationship with the Three in One, and *then* amongst yourselves.

"It is all there ever was, is, or ever shall be."

"Wow…that right there, that was powerful Buddy…"

"Yes, it *IS*. Beyond your wildest imaginings, my dear… In any event, regardless of where the triple filter test originated, it is the most critical key to human interaction."

"Really?'

He nodded.

"I mean, I get what you said about the perfection of God's love and all, but this side of heaven, you expect me to believe that all the problems of the entire human race can be distilled down, and solved by adhering to just those three rules?"

He nodded again.

She snorted. "Dream on Buddy. Maybe where you come from, in Verndari-land it's some kind of paradise, but here on earth, everything's just not that black and white. Life is gray, like ashy elbow and ankle gray, and way more complicated than that."

"And that, is the biggest misconception of them all."

"Come again?"

"It doesn't have to be that way. Aside from artificial divisions, you attach complications, conditions, create disfunction, discord, and drama where there should be none. Were it not for that, trust me, your lives would be far simpler."

"Nope, sorry, I don't buy it," she gave a vigorous shake of her head. "Say what you like, but there isn't a man, who's ever walked this planet who hasn't had to lie to get through a conversation, or situation at one time, or another."

He glanced her way, then looked up. Gazed at something she wished she could see because of his expression just then.

Utter joy.

"Well…there was this one man, you know… A very long time ago…" He turned back to her. Gave her a look that brought her directly to a very spiritual place, for the second time that day.

They shared a knowing smile.

"Fine. Fair enough. But for the rest of us mere mortals, I just don't see it." She shrugged. "Okay, so here's an oldie, but goodie. The absolute classic go-to when it comes to how difficult communication can get. A wife's getting dressed up to go out, and asks her husband, "Honey, do these pants make me look fat?" He looks at her. Who knows? Maybe she looks great, but maybe…just maybe, those pants make her butt look like she just ate Australia for dinner, with a side of New Zealand."

He laughed out loud, and shook his head, as she grinned.

"Now *that*, was a good one. I'll grant you that." He waved his forefinger at her and continued chuckling. "Very funny, that was."

"So, he could be kind. Sure. And say, "why, no

sugar-lips, of course not." But then he'd be lying. Through his teeth. So, you tell me. How in the heck does he apply those rules if he wants to stay happily married?"

"Well, first off, I'd ask why should it matter? And, what's making her ask that question, in the first place? Some societal-imposed beauty standard? Granted, it's not ideal for her to be a size that would endanger her health. But still, all that she is, or will ever be, that's of any consequence at all, is on the inside of her. Where it **counts**. Nothing of that nature is external.

"So, his answer, should reflect his absolute and unequivocal belief in, appreciation for, and acceptance of, that fact. Grounded in a love that demonstrates to her that in the eyes of lovers, everything is beautiful. And whatever the case, he *sees her*. I mean really sees her, and knows quite simply that she matters. To him, specifically. And to the world, more widely.

"His answer, therefore, is his profession of love – necessary, honest, and kind."

"Okay." She considered his words, then grasped his arm for a moment. "I hear what you're saying. But in that case, he's not actually answering what she asked, though, is he? It's a straight question. It requires a straight yes or no response."

"Who says? I put it to you that her question is at its core asking for love, and acceptance, and validation, so any response that addresses *that* is the right one. She's not asking if she's fat, she's asking – Do you appreciate me? Love me? Does anyone?"

"Wow… I can honestly say that never occurred

to me." She leaned back on the bench. "I mean, I've heard it said, over and over, that love is the answer, but it always sounded like such a cliché. Until now. You've literally made a connection in my mind that's real and so relatable. Oh, I def need to write about this in one of my posts." Her mind spun with a host of things. "Like the fact that Verndari believe in God and yet still fail on so many levels when it comes to common moral decency?" She got set to engage her note-taker's AI, her mind already clicking with ideas for how she could tie it all into her unveiling of their soulless agenda.

"You want to write about this, good on you. Spread the word, by all means, but as you do so, might I also suggest you make your actions speak every bit as loudly as your words?" He pierced her with a direct gaze. "In essence... Don't just talk about God, Ms. Sparks. BE about God."

Bemused and very grateful for the turn of events that had brought them to this pivotal point in their interactions, she nodded, as she vowed to give it all some prayerful thought.

"So, back to your original concern. We took a bit of a circuitous route I know, but about this fellow... Dax, is it?"

She nodded.

"So, you say he keeps popping up. He's easy on the eyes, dashing, funny, and all that. How's his demeanor towards you, in particular?"

"In a word, confrontational. It feels like everything I do, or say, he's gotta one-up me. If we'd just met for the first time, or actually liked each other, I'd think he was trying to impress me, or something.

But knowing him as I do, it's just infuriating.

"God alone knows why, but he kept my number. Plus, he asked me, and like a gigantic dummy, I told him, so now he knows where I live too. Would you believe every night, after we leave Dani's place, he calls me? I guess with all the traffic apps he can figure how long it takes me to get there? It's normally pretty late, just after I get to my apartment. He always says he's just checking to see that I made it home safely. Like, stalker much? Then, he wishes me good night and just hangs up. I mean, who does that?"

"I'd say someone who cares about you."

"And so would I, normally, if it were anyone else. But this is Dax Newton we're talking about. Oh, there's an ulterior motive there somewhere. I just know it."

"And what about you? How do you comport yourself when you meet him?"

"Oh, I'm combative, no doubt. I see him coming and my hackles go up, I mean like all the way up, from the get-go. I'm getting armed for battle. Ready for anything, yuh know?" She did a couple quick air punches and upper cuts, like she'd learned in the boxing-for-fitness classes she'd taken a while back. "I'm ready to give him the old one-two."

"Hmm… I see, yes, very graphic. Thank you for that."

His face broke into a wide grin.

"What?"

"You seriously don't see it, do you?"

"Duh…obviously not. So, why don't you enlighten me?"

"And enlighten I shall. Tell me, has it occurred

to you that he's simply reacting to the energy in the room? Quite literally defending himself, against your – 'come any closer and I shall pop you one, in the face. Quite viciously really, and repeatedly, and at the very least until you're picking your teeth up off this *fabtastic* linoleum flooring,' type of energy?"

"Really?"

He threw his head back and roared with laughter this time.

"Those were just verbal confrontation metaphors, Buddy. Seriously? I cannot believe you. Get a grip man, for heaven's sake."

All joking aside, she thought about it for a minute, and pictures of Newton's quirky smile turning into a scowl after she hit him with a zinger, or gave him a look intended to whither, flashed through her mind.

"So, what you're saying is this is all my fault? That I'm the reason why he treated me the way he did? Is that it?"

"No, certainly not. Well, not entirely at any rate. You haven't said what led to your original impasse. But what I'd like is for you to just consider the possibility that perhaps you may be contributing a tad more than you think, to whatever it is that's perpetuating and fueling the hostility between you…*now*."

"Mm-mm…no way, this goes way deeper than that. You don't know what he did. I didn't ask for it, and I certainly didn't deserve to be treated that way."

"Fair enough." He held up his hands. "But can I inveigle you to have a bit of a chat, at least, from a brand-new perspective…hmm?" He gave her an expectant look.

"So, necessary, honest and kind. Oh, and don't hurt anyone. Check and check. Yeah, I gotcha. Gonna be kinda one-sided though, wouldn't it be? Unless you're planning to do your little trick and pop up at his place to have this same convo with him." She smiled, joking, but maybe just a teensy bit hopeful. She eyed him. "You aren't, are you?"

"No, of course not. I expect you'll manage well enough by working on yourself first. Let the change begin with you, Ms. Sparks." He rose from the bench. "You want to talk clichés? Well now, I believe that's the truest of them all. Stay safe and blessed as always, my intrepid reporter."

He smiled, touched his forehead in gallant salute, turned on his heel, and kept up a brisk pace as he crossed the street, walked around the corner, and disappeared from her view.

Chapter 9

Matthew 24:11
And many false prophets shall rise, and shall
deceive many…

My fellow skeptical Americans…
How's this for a cliché?
Some readers of these posts are clapping
back. Asking me to give our resident 'saviors' the
benefit of the doubt. Saying they're just different,
bankrupt, when it comes to the currency of
human culture, so they can't be held accountable
for any 'lapses' in diplomacy.
Lapses? Seriously?
Let's run the list, shall we? They value
their privacy to the exclusion of all else. Does
that really excuse away their unwillingness to be

forthcoming with the public about their activities, not just in America, but around the world?

They're not open to interviews, or unscripted questions from the media. They only give responses they've prepared in advance. They almost never mix with humans, preferring the company of their own kind. Yet still, they all but control the progression, direction, and content of both social and mainstream media that's exclusively for human consumption.

They've been called condescending in some quarters because they've publicly professed to being in the top 1% of the world's most wealthy, they say, due entirely to their superiority to humans. They have controlling interests in some of the world's largest financial institutions. Yet, word has it that they're thick as thieves with nearly every oligarch and billionaire in the world, so who's bank rolling who? And how's this for the icing on the cake? I have it on good authority that contrary to popular belief, they aren't atheists at all, and instead acknowledge the existence of a good and moral God, even if their actions totally belie that fact.

So, you tell me, do those sound like the qualities and actions of beings who'd have OUR best interests at heart, as they claim?

Are they anxious to integrate? Assimilate? Or God forbid, are they really here to dominate & annihilate?

My guys out there and my ladies. When's the last time a potential partner said "I'm a super private person so, don't call. Don't text. In fact,

I'd really prefer you not ask me anything at all because I don't credit you with having the intelligence, or the net worth, to hang with me. But hey, on the bright side, you can trust me with all your cash."

And you said – "Great, that wasn't suspicious at all. I've been waiting for you my whole life, so what should we get Sushi, or Italian tnite?"

You decide.
Till next time, anxious to hear from you.
Cynical in NYC

Digital Dante

Hey, I read your last couple posts. All good points that are sure to attract some attention. You're really going for the jugular now, aren't you. Speaking of which, you prob'ly think I'm killing the Dante quotes, 😄 *but from my reading, I just keep seeing so many parallels between what you're writing about the defenders right now, and his treatise on the ills of his time.*

You see, at its core, Inferno was about how sin contributes to social disorder. And within the discussion of the major sins, naturally there are sociopolitical overtones. He shined a bright spotlight on the decline in trust in institutions and the authorities who abused their positions and exploited the people. Purporting to be working for them while serving their own selfish interests

What really struck me was the way he

showed how truly insidious the little things are, that people just gloss over, not realizing how they eat away at the very fabric of society. Bit by bit, over time. To say nothing of the post-truth culture, where facts get replaced by carefully scripted talking points, and so-called alternative facts. Dante wrote – "Reason flies, when following the senses, on clipped wings."

So, have we ignored the signs? Let good sense get chased away, or buried? Acted on uninformed instinct, or suasion, to the point where we could lose our most basic freedoms?

The remaining democratic territories in the world, some would say strongholds, are steadily giving over to creeping fascism and defender, slash, oligarch-controlled structures of government. Kinda makes you wonder, what truly sinister things have the defenders and the authorities that support them already done, that we as a country, and as a world, have just ignored?

So, all that to say, I did a deep dive. If you really wanna poke some holes in their fake 'savior' persona and draw attention to how the powers that be are either turning a blind eye, or are downright complicit, check out this research paper I uncovered. It's from a student at Yale. It delves into the real impact of some of the initiatives they've introduced. Oh, and make sure you're sitting down when you do.

BTW this next quote I remembered, it's not about them.

This one's just for you... 😊

"There is a gentle thought that often springs to life in me because it speaks of you."
Till next time, Ms. Cynic.

Chapter 10

Job 41:22
In his neck remaineth strength, and sorrow is
turned into joy before him…

Marly felt some of her very best memories from childhood spring to life, as she walked along the narrow path at the back of her apartment complex, leading to the residents' outdoor pool.

It wasn't maintained to a standard she considered adequate, so unfortunately, she hardly ever used it. She'd always wait until the day right after the cleaning company came and put in the required chemicals and raked out all the fallen leaves from the surrounding trees. And even then, if any of the residents' children got there ahead of her, she'd give it a pass. They could be quite a handful. Even though there was always a teenager or two around, ostensibly to supervise, she always wound up consoling one of the smaller ones, with gentle words, while tending to a scraped knee. Or trying to quiet a temper tantrum. Or, watching with her heart in her throat, as they executed some maneuver off the diving board that could quite easily land them in the emergency room.

She got to the entrance and looked in. Not a soul. Fantastic! She'd have the place all to herself. She waved a hand across the security screen that kept out non-resident trespassers, and waited until the energy shield slid down and disappeared, before stepping through.

It really was such a beautiful day out. Putting her hand up to shield her eyes from the glare, she squinted at the gorgeous blue sky. Not a cloud in sight. Feeling the heat of the sun-warmed pavers beneath her bare feet, she walked to the deep end and leaned down. Admired the pretty azure tiling that made the pool such a gorgeous bright turquoise. Smelt the faint hint of chlorine as she ran a hand back and forth into the crystal-clear water. It was the perfect temperature too, warmed enough by the daytime heat to remove the night's chill, but still cool enough to be refreshing on such a hot summer day.

Not wanting to waste time, since any of the kids could turn up soon, she tugged off her towel. Threw it onto a nearby deckchair, closed her eyes and jumped right in, feet first. Ahh, the delicious sensation of the water enfolding her as she sunk down into its welcoming depths. Waving her arms in a back-and-forth motion that would take her back up to the surface, she opened her eyes.

And found herself surrounded.

By gloomy grey.

In an instant, the water turned cold, and something grasped her right leg, encircling it in an even icier clasp. Struggling, she reached down, tried to claw at whatever had her in tight grip, but instead felt only the dull scrape of her fingernails against her own leg. Frantic, she tried again to use her arms and to kick her legs as hard as she could to free herself. She even summoned up a burst of her flying power to try to propel her back to the surface, but still she was ensnared, and running out of air.

Normally she knew when she was in the void, hemmed in by illusions, but this time was different. This time she'd walked right into a beautiful memory and not recognized her peril. There'd been a pool at the very first apartment she'd rented years earlier. But there wasn't one where she was living now. How had her mind become so clouded, she didn't even realize she was being lured into a watery trap?

Oh God, help me…

She felt her heart pounding out of her chest. And unable to hold her breath for a second longer, her lungs forced her to inhale, and to her shock, what she took into them wasn't drowning liquid.

It was air.

Blessed, even if slightly moldy smelling, air.

She could still feel the wet, cold pressure and resistance of water around her as she continued to use her arms and legs to try to free herself, but thankfully at least, she could breathe.

She closed her eyes again, felt a moment's relief that was short lived, as an even stronger tug on her leg of whatever had her, began pulling her down faster. Much further and deeper, to where it was growing progressively darker and colder. She renewed her struggles, even trying to shake herself awake, and instead of waving her arms around at her waist, she reached up above her head, trying to get enough momentum to bring her arms down with force, in hopes of dislodging her icy bonds.

She looked up.

Something disturbed the depths above her.

It was her angel.

His massive wings were stirring the water with energy. She felt a faint vibration ripple towards her. His warm, strong hand grasped her left arm and in scant seconds he pulled her up, right past him, to the surface. She gasped as she broke through. Looked straight up at a stunning, bright blue sky as the sheer force of her explosive emergence propelled her way up into the sunny, open air, high above the water.

She slowed her decent, floated down, and then landed.

Perfectly balanced. On a smooth, solid surface, that bobbed gently up and down beneath her bare feet.

Taking in a deep, cleansing breath, she closed her eyes, passed a hand over her face, and then along her hair. Felt the cool water splash from it, onto her neck, down her chest and the center of her back. Opening her eyes again, she looked down and then around.

Her bathing suit was gone. In its place she was wearing a shiny, navy wet suit, and was perched on a very large, oval-shaped board. It was beautiful. Artfully splashed with black, bright green, and yellow paint, and with the word MOBAY printed in big, bold, white letters at its very center.

Afloat on a spectacular azure ocean.

Off in the distance she could just make out its frothy swells rolling into a pristine, white-sand, tropical beach, dotted here and there with clusters of palm trees. A sudden cooling breeze ruffled her hair, caressed her face with a refreshing touch. And even from this far away she could hear the soothing, nearly musical rustling of the palm fronds on their branches, and the lapping sound of the waves rolling into shore.

"No dancing today."

She heard her angel's deep, melodic voice around her head, as his weight landed on the board, tilting it back a bit at her feet.

She grinned. Welcoming his comforting presence right behind her. Then let out a little shriek, as he grasped her waist and they shot forward, skimming along the surface of the water at high speed, heading towards the shore.

The feeling was exhilarating, beyond her very wildest dreams. She could smell the salt of the sea spray, tasted it on her lips, as a brisk breeze whipped her hair around her head. Tilting her face up, she felt the blessed warmth of the sun kiss her skin.

All too soon, they glided in close to the sand. Thinking that the ride was over she was about to protest, but gasped instead, and grabbed his right hand at her waist. Gripped his thumb, as they made a sharp turn and accelerated sideways, skirting all along the length of the endless shoreline.

They made a sudden wide arc then, away from the beach, heading back out into the ocean. Even with his firm, reassuring hold on her waist and her grip on his hand, she was still swung forward, slid onto her tiptoes and nearly off the motorized board with the force of their change in direction. Reflexively she used her bare toes to grip its edge. Tilted all the way forward, she reveled in the thrilling sensation of being nearly parallel to the ocean's surface. Stuck the fingers of her free hand in and felt the intense pleasure of the water churning around them, as they completed the sharp curve.

Going backwards now, she straightened as they were swept along. Lost her breath as they hit a sudden large swell, and as they were lifted steadily higher, she took a quick peak over her shoulder. Felt a heady mix of excitement and terror at the sight of an immensely high tunnel of captivating blue water topped by white foam, forming right behind them.

"Uh-oh. Wipe out!" her angel shouted on a burst of laughter. Just before they were bumped up suddenly and bucked right off the board.

She shrieked in joy as she flew forward and up into the air. She did a somersault, caught sight of the bright yellow sun and then closed her eyes and held her nose, as she felt the wall of foamy water hit her from all sides, as her feet plunged into the accommodating ocean.

"Oh!" She awoke to the sound of her delighted gasp.

Grinning, she let out a loud whooping sound. Gave thanks as always for the new day, and on that particular morning, for new beginnings. Realizing that while she'd previously dreaded going to sleep, now she felt almost eager for the nights to come.

And as she lay there in silence, but for the pounding of her pulse in her ears and feeling the thrumming excitement fade to a dull tingle, she sent a further little prayer of thanksgiving heavenward.

Thank you, Father, for my guardian angel, and for turning my very worst nightmares, into my very best dreams…

And as she wondered what new and exciting adventure bedtime would bring, she rose, anxious to face the day ahead.

And that night…

My fellow skeptical Americans…

Let's talk about unpublicized weapons tech. This cynic has it on good authority that nearly every supposed innocuous advancement in defender generated tech has a deadly counterpart in the form of alternate and strategic military application. Sources say that in the bowels of the Verndari Diplomatic Center, behind military-grade energy shields, there've been undisclosed weapons tests. For explosive devices that would make what happened in New Atlantis in 2120 look like a scratch bomb went off, by comparison. There's even secret footage of a sub-basement level 'oven', and I use the term loosely because I'm told, aside from an off-the-charts, degree of heat, and looking like it could go nuclear at any moment, it also gives off an awful, putrid stench. When pressed, defenders claimed it's used for their version of meal preparation.

Really?

I don't know a darn thing about Verndari cuisine, but I'm willing to bet whatever they're cooking up down there, is not for their consumption.

Now prepare yourself, some of the footage is really disturbing, I know, but we need to see it. We need to be disturbed, and shook up, and yes, terrified, if that's what it takes to raise awareness, swing the tide, and bring about real change.

The truth is out there, people. You only have to look.

So here goes nothing.

Click on the links below for more if you dare. And if you care. About your family, your fellowman, and our future as a great nation.

And as always...

You decide.

Till next time, anxious to hear from you.

Cynical in NYC

Chapter 11

Psalms 46:10
Be still, and know that I am God…

"Come on Marly, you can do this… It's just like Buddy says, right? – "Nothing ventured, nothing gained." Well, here goes nothing." She blew out a shaky breath and nodded so her screen AI would start texting her words.

Dante. Do you have a minute?

She waited a couple anxious minues, but got no response. Disappointed, she was about to close her air screen when –
DING.

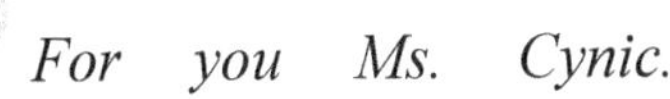

Always.

She beamed. Rolled her shoulders to try to rid them of some nervous tension and started speaking again.

Hey, thanks for responding. I'm really glad you're online tnite. I wanted to thank you again for the weapons footage you sent me the other day. It really put the icing on the cake of what I'd already gathered on my end.

Sure. I got you. Good looking out BTW. That basement barbecue is hands down, just the freakiest crap I've ever seen. My sources say they've had to go to ground and halt some of their activities since that last post. Human rights groups and even ecclesiastical associations are beginning to put real pressure on the powers that be to investigate and tell people what's been going on. You're really doing it. You're reaching over a million people and turning the tide, and not just in the US. Good for you Ms.Cynic. I knew you could do it. 😉

Wow. That vote of confidence means a whole lot, coming from you.

She drew in a deep breath.

Speaking of which, I've been meaning to talk to you. I've been getting some fatherly counselling from an older friend of mine on how I can grow both personally and professionally from all of this. And suffice it to say, he laid out some guidelines for me, so, I've been trying to meet the triple filter test as far as possible with what I say. You know, to say only what is necessary, honest and kind. So, in the spirit of growth, in the honesty department, here goes – these last two months we've been texting have been really surprising. In a good way. And I don't just mean because of all the progress we've made bringing awareness to The Defender Agenda. I feel like we've made a real personal connection, so I want to tell you, I like you, Dante. A lot. And I've been wondering, also a whole lot 😁 how you feel about me, on a personal level.

You don't really know who I am though. Do you? Have you considered, I could be a serial killer, for all you know? Just luring you in. Waiting for an opportunity to pounce and add your skin to my latest epidermal suit, or your body parts to the growing collection in my freezer. 😋 😆

Well, I haven't read any cases of serial killers who claim Dante as their inspiration in life and in murder, so I think I'll take my chances. 😊 Besides, I think I've got your number, Sir Poet. I know nearly everything I need to know about you already. Just from your texts.

 *Oh, really? And what's that?*

Well, let's see…You're super smart, and funny, and spontaneous. You're a person of great faith. I can tell, from the reverence you attach, whenever you talk about God. I can see just how important He is in your life.

Oh, and you couldn't even spell out the phrase 'bitch-slap' when we first started texting.

That tells me you use your words to uplift, to amuse, and to edify, and not to curse.

You're generous. When you give of yourself and your time there are no half-measures. You're all in.

You're chivalrous, always ready and willing to aid a damsel in distress, in her righteous cause. I'm def testimony to that.

And Dante's writings… well, I think they move you. I think you have the kindred soul of a poet, and his words feed that very best part of you. They're an integral piece of your moral compass and they make you a better man. The wonderful, phenomenal man that you are.

That's what I think.

So, what say you? How'd I do?

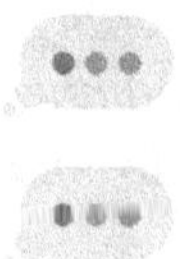

I'll tell you what I think. I think one good turn deserves another. So, shall I tell you what I've learned about you in these last couple months?

Sure, go ahead. I'm all ears.

You're sweet and quirky and you're a strong woman of faith, sometimes thrown by life's battles, but always poised to rally and to reach for ultimate success, no matter the odds. You love to laugh, you're compassionate, bright, and sensitive. But you're stubborn. Gets you in trouble often I'd bet because sometimes you're intentions are misunderstood. Plus, you won't back down from a challenge, or your point of view. Especially if you believe you're in the right.

You get emotional, angry sometimes, but it's because you loathe injustice and want to leave the world a better place than how you found it. You're passionate, about any and every righteous cause, and I think you're that way in your personal life as well. And I think that anyone who's blessed enough to be in your orbit should thank God and their lucky stars for being there. And they should respect and cherish you, like the queen you are.

That. Is what I think.

She took a moment to read his heart-stopping words again. Lingered on and absorbed every nuanced sylable.

Wow… I'm stunned. I don't even know what to say right now, except, thank you.

 *So, don't say anything. You don't need to. Why not just be quiet in this moment.*

It's like Dante said – "Everywhere is here and every when is now." I've always thought it a potent reminder that with all the craziness in the world around us, all the time. Sometimes it's OK to just live, and embrace who, and where we are in time. And in God. To enjoy. To thrive. Or even just exist. Like we're doing… Right here. And right now. In this very poignant, exquisite moment.

Till next time, Ms. Cynic.

"Till next time, Dante," she whispered after he clicked off.

Waving a hand over her air screen to shut it off, she fell back in her chair.

She felt so many emotions coming to the fore in the moment he'd just created for her, and now.

Pleasure, at his intriguing, and yes, gratifying, characterization of her. A mixture of excitement and apprehension, over what the future could hold for them. Satisfaction, that she'd put herself out there for the very first time in her life, in telling him how much she liked him.

But last of all came the disturbing and lingering discouragement, when she took a moment to recognize–

That he…hadn't actually said it back.

Chapter 12

Proverbs 18:2
A fool hath no delight in understanding, but that his
heart may discover itself...

"So, how are things progressing with your young man. Had that little honest chit-chat yet, and what did he say back?"

"I thought we agreed from now on when we meet on this bench, we should focus on our priority of getting the word out about the defenders?"

"But we've got that covered for today. Your viewership just crossed the milestone million mark. And you know exactly what you're going to post tonight, don't you?"

She nodded.

"Well, there you go. And by the way, *you* agreed. Unilaterally. While I, on the other hand, said I still think you need to resolve your issues, *if* you really wish to grow personally, as a person of faith, and as a young successful professional."

She sighed.

"Nothing's "progressing" as you put it, and like I said before, he's not *my* anything. Plus, that's really none of your business anyway, Buddy, so I'll thank you to mind your own affairs."

"Been looking at those old '*Ace Ventura*' movies again, have we?"

"Well, yeah…but no. That was actually my imitation of a British saying. Didn't I get the accent right?"

"Not even a smidge."

"Really? I thought that one was pretty good."

"I'm sure you did."

"Guess I'll just have to keep practicing."

"Well, good luck with that."

"Yuh know, I've read that the defenders speak all of earth's languages, fluently. I've heard a few of them speak English and it sounded to me like they all had different accents. I guess from how, or where they learnt to speak it? So, what about you? Where'd you learn? Was it in England?"

He gave her a blank look.

"Have you ever even *been* to the UK?"

"Off and on."

"And there he goes, being all vague-a-licious again."

"I beg your pardon?"

"Oh, it's something my friend Dani says to describe a good-looking guy who's all mysterious. Like what she says about your friend, Svikari? Well, she'd say buff and tasty, and mysterious, but you get the idea."

He barked out a laugh. "Svikari? Buff and tasty? And she's actually used *those* very words… To his face?"

"Yeah, all the time, the way she tells it."

"Oh, now that is just priceless, that is," he laughed again. "I do believe I'd enjoy meeting her sometime. She sounds like a riot. Positively delightful."

"You have no idea."

"So, shall we get back to your…uh…this Dax fellow."

"Uhhg," she half growled and groaned. "Do we have to?"

"Certainly not, but there's quite obviously lingering resentment and negativity there you need to let go of, and I promised I'd help you be your best self. So, come along. We know you're positively gutted by what happened. That you think whatever he did in the past was despicable. I dare say, diabolical. But what about now?"

"Now, I'm not so sure I'm even interested in him, or care, either way anymore. Lately I've been texting with this other guy. Remember the truther I mentioned? Who follows my underground posts and has been sending me useful research info? Well, I know we've never met face to face, but he is absolutely amazing. I can't explain it, but I feel this connection between us. It's like I know him. We just click. It's kinda like how I felt about Newton when we first met. Before things went south between us. It's like I'm back on cloud nine again. It's getting so that I keep checking my feed all day to see if he's messaged, and then late at night to see if maybe he's online, so we can talk some more. Just the other night, he described how he sees me, and he painted this incredible picture. Newton would *never* do something like that. It was thoughtful, and sensitive, and lovely. I mean, you'd think he'd try to say only nice stuff to get on my good side, but instead it was this complex, balanced, nuanced portrait. It was real, but yet still so flattering."

"Are you sure you're not just projecting some repressed positive impressions and feelings you had for Dax onto this other more accessible and affable fellow?"

"No. Of course not. Why would you say that? He's an entirely different person."

"Is he though? In your mind? Because from what you just said, it seems like you're comparing the two of them and how they measure up, quite a bit, really."

"No, I'm not. Wait… Am I?"

"Alright. Let's try something, shall we? Close your eyes."

"Seriously? Why?"

"Just humor me and do it, will you?"

"Fine," she huffed and let her eyelids close down.

"Now, I want you to clear your mind and just listen to the sound of my voice. Focus on your breathing. Inhale deeply… Hold it. Good…now breathe out, slowly. Again. In… Hold… and breathe out. And again…one last time…

"Brilliant. Now, I want you to picture the absolute, hands down, best time you've had in the last…oh…say, two weeks. See yourself sifting through your memories and then really latching onto the one you want, in your mind. Can you see it?"

"Yeah."

"Good. Now, describe it to me."

"I'm having dinner at my friend Dani and her husband Joe's home. I never miss a chance to spend time with them. They're both such incredible people, and boy, oh boy, do they know how to entertain. They've got it going on! The Michelin star-quality food, the music, the old movies and TV, and the great conversation. Plus, she's got the best sense of humor of anyone I know. I always have such a great time. Well, except for Insufferable of course."

"Sorry, who?"

"Oh, Newton. That's just what I call him."

"What? To his face? And you still think the hostility between you two is all his fault? Hi, keep those eyes closed. I didn't say you could open them just yet."

"Well, of course not to his face. It's just a private thing." She closed her eyes again. "The word just popped into my head years ago and kinda stuck. Truth is, even if I wanted to, and I'm not saying I do, I doubt I could get it out of my head at this point."

"Right, so get centered again."

She did the breathing exercise, all on her own this time.

"So, you're having dinner at your friend Dani's. I want you to picture the eye-catching culinary creation on the table, smell the delicious aromas. That lovely music you like so much is playing in the background, and you're all having a smashing time.

Can you feel yourself there? Immersed in all those lovely sensations?"

She nodded.

"Good. Now where's Dax?"

"He's sitting right across the table from me. Where he always sits. Prob'ly so I'll have a perfect ringside seat to see his arrogant, smug face, when he frowns and smirks at me."

"I see…so forget him for the moment. Think about something Dani said that was funny. Do you remember anything?"

"Yeah, she told us about a case she was on where she had to "school a perp" in her words," she snorted at the memory. "She pretended like she was crazy, pointed her gun at his head and asked him if he wanted to test her. Or keep on breathing. I mean to hear her tell it. You would just split a side. I laughed so hard my eyes were watering. I remember I even thanked her. Told her I hadn't laughed like that in years."

"Now look across at Dax. What's he doing just then?"

"He's laughing too, like there's no tomorrow. He looks so good too. His entire face, it just transforms and lights up when he smiles, or laughs, yuh know?"

"And did he *say* anything?"

"Yeah, to me actually… he said, "For real, Marly. I was just thinking that same thing. It's so good to see you laugh like that…again…"

"Oh…"

Her eyes snapped open.

"Oh wow, I'd totally forgot that."

"Yes, I should say so. Right, let's review all of that, shall we? First off, don't you find it curious that when I asked you to pick your very best memory, it wasn't one with the amazing truther, but instead, your sub-conscious led you directly to one with your dear friends, and Dax?"

"Wow. I have to say, you're freakin' me out just a little bit right now, Buddy. How did you learn to do that? That, was like Psychology 101, right there. And I see what you're saying. I didn't even think of Dante."

"Who's this now?"

"The truther. Try to keep up, will yuh? It's his online handle."

"Oh, well naturally, what else would it be?" His lips compressed on a slight smile.

"I mean, five minutes ago if you'd asked, I would have said Newton never has a single good thing to say to me. But now, I think maybe I've been so mad I've just been blocking out of my mind, all the good stuff that happens during our interactions."

"See? So, in that moment, thinking back, would you describe him as, oh, I don't know, 'agreeable' at least?"

"Yeah, I guess."

"So, there you go. I'd say you've turned an important corner. You said you couldn't stop thinking of him as insufferable, but now, rather than trying to stop thinking the negative word, you've instead successfully created a positive alternative in your mind, to reinforce a new way of thinking. Bravo! Good for you! I knew you could do it. Yes. The heart wants what the heart wants, Ms. Sparks, and I think we both know where yours is leading you."

"Wait, just hold on a minute there, Buddy. Just because I've become aware of some random good stuff in our latest exchanges, doesn't by any means negate his sins of the past. I'm still plenty mad about that. It just comes bubbling back up every time I see him. And sure, I might have forgiven him as part of my faith journey, but no matter what you say, I'm still not sure I could ever get over that hurt and how awful he made me feel."

"Well, at least promise me you'll keep an open mind about the present circumstance, as you work through whatever it is in your past that's so much of a hurdle for you."

"Fair enough."

He nodded, and she actually felt pretty good about their entire exchange.

At least until–

"Brilliant! Say what you like. I've still got a very good feeling about you two. Mark my words. It won't be long now, till you're both blissfully in love. Married. Collaborating. Connecting. Blending. You know… vigorously bumping hips, and dangly bits, and such?"

"Oh. My. God! Seriously, Buddy?! Are you kidding me right now?! Like what the actual hell?!"

A rather delicious picture flashed through her mind…

"Wait…"

And then another…

"…Really? I mean… Yuh think so?"

"You are most welcome." He grinned.

My fellow skeptical Americans…

I grant you; it's no secret the defenders brought with them significant advancements to our civilization.

In medicine – they've pushed us forward decades as it relates to how science understands human physiology and medical treatment at a cellular level. Further than we probably could have ever gone on our own in the last 25 years.

But remember when we talked about their secret weapons tech? Would it surprise you to learn they're using that very knowledge about human anatomy to engineer new laser weapons that can initiate spontaneous human combustion? Capable of reducing a human body to ash in mere seconds? How long do you think it will be before every warring nation, terrorist group and neighborhood gang turn those devastating weapons on an unsuspecting and entirely unprepared population?

In social outreach – there's free junk food in nearly every neighborhood, so no one goes hungry, but question – just how damaging are the synthetic foods those machines dispense? Research statistics show that in those last nearly three decades since they arrived, obesity, diabetes, heart disease, strokes, and other lifestyle diseases, have all increased exponentially. Coincidence? Click on the links below if you don't believe me.

See for yourself.

And then ask yourself – are they prolonging

lives, or systematically stripping it away from all humanity? One inner city single parent and kid at a time.

And what do they really mean, by their new slogan "let us help you." Maybe we should be asking, help us do what?

You decide.

Till next time, anxious to hear from you.

Cynical in NYC

Chapter 13

Hebrews11:30
By faith the walls of Jericho fell down, after they
were compassed about seven days…

"Here, let me help you."

Insufferable…or rather, Agreeable…rushed to step ahead of her and then turned back, as he reached her car.

After yet another incredibly delicious meal. The second in nearly as many days that week. They'd just walked to where their cars were parked, a fair distance apart on Dani and Joe's circular driveway, to the right of the house.

It was pretty late, since Dani's case load on days like this one kept her so long, the four of them, without Rissa and Duncan this time, had met for supper, rather than dinner. Still, such a welcome diversion from the many and varied stresses of life.

And speaking of pains in her butt…

He flashed her a dashing smile.

And she tried to remember Buddy's plea of the week before to keep an open mind. It was certainly proving to be a challenge.

"No worries. Just relax. I got you," the deep, overtly sexy tone of his voice sounded just a bit contrived as he extended a hand towards her car door.

She pasted on a smile and resisted the urge to roll her eyes.

"That's not necessary. I assure you, I'm perfectly capable of opening it on my own, thank you. After all, I've only been doing it, *alone*, for the last ten years."

He let out a low exasperated growl.

Her gaze snapped to his.

"I was just trying to do something nice for you, Marly. Dang! I thought this would blow over soon, given the number of times we've been around each other in the last month, but you really don't give a bad-devil-damn, if this…whatever the hell this is…just drags on forever, do you?!"

Annoyance aside, she almost laughed, since if they'd been good friends, she would have enjoyed sharing a joke with him over how much Dani and her cute little humorous and always colorful expressions were starting to rub off on him.

Instead, she glared, as he scowled.

Defiant, she held his angry gaze. Gave back every bit as good as she got. Waved the door open herself, as she got level with him, then turned to her car.

"Okay, that's it." With a flick of his wrist, the

door swished closed again. He grasped her upper arm and swung her back around to face him. "This has gone way past far enough, so time to tell me. Exactly what did I do to you, to warrant this level of hostility, huh?"

He searched her eyes.

"Seriously? You're kidding me, right?" She snatched her arm away and narrowed her gaze on him.

"What?! For God's sake, talk to me! 'Cause trust me, I genuinely have no clue what's happening right now. Every time we meet here for a meal, I feel like I should ask Joe to hide his knives, and Dani if I can borrow something of hers that's made from Kevlar." He chuckled as his face lit up with a dashing grin.

"Oh, don't give me that Prince Charming routine. I fell for it once, but I promise you I wo–" She took in a deep breath, realizing she'd already said too much.

Dammit Marly...

She felt her face heat and tried to turn to her car, so she could just leave.

"Oh no." He stopped her again. This time with both hands, on both of her arms. He peered down at her, his deep brown eyes intense in the dim light. "What do you mean, you fell for it once?" His voice softened. "When exactly did you fall for me? Is that what this is about?"

"You really don't know?"

He shook his head, and she absorbed and accepted the genuine look of confusion imprinted on his face.

She took in a shaky breath, as a picture of

Buddy's sincere blue eyes and handsome face saying the words 'complete honesty', flashed through her mind.

"It was that first year we were both at G and R, okay? Remember we worked for over three weeks on that great interview at NASA, the one on the new family space program they were launching, when they first started sending entire families into space?"

"Yeah, of course, that assignment was amazing."

"I thought so too, and not just because the story was so great, but because it felt like we really clicked, professionally and…uh…personally."

"And that's exactly how I felt, but then you got so cold, right after. I just figured you didn't feel the same way."

"Well, not right after. Once we wrapped, you asked if I'd wanna go out sometime. You remember?"

"Yeah, of course. I was really looking forward to it too."

"And I…was on cloud nine. I mean, I don't think my feet even touched the floor for the rest of that day. Well, until that night…"

She paused, not sure she wanted to go to a place that had caused her so much bitterness and pain. She'd spent a whole lot of nights praying to just let it all go. Maybe this wasn't such a good idea after all, maybe–

"Come on Marly, we've come this far. Go on. Please?"

Something in his eyes moved her. And more than that, his soft-spoken words, as he said a word she'd never heard before, in the context of a relationship. From him, or from any other man she'd ever encountered,

He'd said "we."

And for her, that was a definite game changer.

"Okay… so, that same night I stayed to work late, and I heard you talking to Brad in the breakroom."

His brows drew together. His face – a picture of concentration. At least until it fell. "What exactly did you hear?" He released his hold on her arms.

"What didn't I hear, you mean." She felt all the anger, hurt, feelings of deep betrayal and resentment she'd bottled up all come bubbling to the surface again. "Like the part where when he asked, you told him you didn't really have any interest in me. Oh…or maybe, what he said next, that he was glad to hear it, given what he had planned for me. All of the many different ways he knew, to get women, but in particular, good, Christian women, to think they'd fallen in love. And him, with them. Like saying he enjoyed going on periodic spiritual retreats to the Benedictine monastery on the mount, or that he couldn't wait to go with them to their church, oh…and of course, that he was only looking for a serious relationship that led to marriage." She shook her head on a bitter laugh. "And then when he described in disgusting detail all he'd do once he got me? I mean, he even said which positions he was gonna use, to dominate, and shame, and show me–" she compressed her lips, unable to continue as the vile words took life in her brain.

"And after that?" His voice was mild, but his jaw

was tight, his expression an unusual mixing of emotions. At once controlled, then enraged, then unreadable.

"What? You don't remember the rest? You want a play by play? Is that it? Well, sorry to disappoint, but I'd heard quite enough by then. I left. So, I could go throw up the dinner I'd just eaten."

He looked distraught at that, gave her a questioning look.

She nodded her confirmation.

Once.

Oh, it had happened all right. Just like she said. She'd been sick to her stomach, for real.

He looked down at the pavers at their feet. When he looked up again, his gaze was focused. His voice somber. Measured.

"I asked because if you'd stayed you would have heard what *I* did and said next."

"Oh, really? Well, what was that? I'm all ears."

"I'm by no means proud of this, but I punched him. Right in his stupid, misogynistic face. More than once. And hard. Think I broke his nose. And while he was on the breakroom floor bleeding, I told him if he ever took God out of his thoughts, to so much as look in your direction. Ever. I'd kick his ass. Again. Only worse next time."

She drew in a quick breath, surprised at his use of language she'd never heard from him before. She crossed her arms over her chest and looked away as she considered his words.

"Then…"

She felt the gentle brush of his finger under her chin as he turned her face, and her gaze back to his.

"Then… I picked his sorry butt up off the floor, helped clean him up, then schooled him. Told him that instead of trying to trick her, he should count himself very fortunate and blessed to ever have a strong woman of faith at his side. To love, support, and pray him through anything. To lift him up in the courts of our God, to such heights of success the likes of which he could never, ever imagine, or achieve on his own."

Stunned at his eloquent declaration, she thought back. Remembered the next day.

She'd glimpsed Brad, his face swollen, bandaged, and his eyes bloodshot. But she'd just figured he'd probably crossed paths with some church girl's big brother, or daddy, and got exactly what was coming to him. He'd practically run in the opposite direction when he saw her, and she'd just thought it a blessing he'd taken her off his sleazy hit list.

Now she knew why.

"And, as for what I said at first, about not being interested in you, well that's on me, I gotta own that, for real." He rubbed a hand over his chin, then through his hair. "I dunno, maybe it was just some macho bull for his benefit – acting young and dumb. Because trust me, mentally, I have never been that immature, *or* that stupid. Ever. I think in that moment, when he asked me if there was anything between us, I def wasn't ready to face my feelings, that's for sure. And then by the time I came to my senses, you pulled away, completely. I couldn't even talk to you. You'd just put up this Kings Hotel-sized wall and got downright–"

"Hostile?"

"Not my words, but yes." He gave her a little smile. "I was gonna say distant, but yeah, I think if you'd had the opportunity with those icy looks you gave me and those biting words, you would have sliced me to the core. A couple times."

"You have no idea…and *that,* isn't the half of it." She leveled a fake look on him, intended to scare him. Then giggled as his face fell. "Wow, you are so easy." She wagged a finger at him and then gave his arm a playful swat. "I'm gonna have to remember that."

She took a look at her watch as an alert popped up. "Okay, well I guess I better go. It's getting late and I've got some writing to do for tomorrow's edition, and for another piece I'm doing, before I turn in." She flipped a couple screens.

"Yeah, sure, but before you go, I feel like we've turned an important corner tonight. Come to a new kind of understanding? Shouldn't we seal the deal? You know, kiss and make up?"

Her gaze snapped to his.

"Uh…or something. To mark the start of a renewed friendship, at least?"

His smile was so adorable, she just couldn't say no.

Plus, if she was honest with herself first, like Buddy recommended, she'd been dying to kiss him all those years ago when they'd first worked together.

And now she knew he wasn't the kind of man she'd mistaken him to be, for all this time, all the barriers to more between them had just come crashing down. Suddenly and unexpectedly, like Jericho's walls.

And oh, she wanted so much to kiss him right then. Even more than before.

But still, not wanting to seem too eager, she got set to play it cool.

He reached out, and she allowed him to turn her, so her back was against her car, even as he stepped forward, hemming her in with his tall frame. He looked down at her, brushed her cheek with gentle fingers as a secret smile moved his lips. "Have I ever told you…you've got the most beautiful green eyes I've ever seen?"

She shook her head, and as she stared up into his steady, bronze ones, she was caught and held.

"They call out to me. Even now, they're like a beacon. And such a welcome balm… I feel them… I can't even explain it…it's like they reach in and touch my soul."

Her heart did a little flip in her chest.

Remember… be cool… her head instructed as she took in a breath.

"Sure, whatever," she exhaled and shrugged.

His left eyebrow popped up. He looked confused and maybe even a little…sad?

But still, he leaned in, unhurried.

She watched his lids begin to lower before closing her eyes. She leaned in as well, let her lips open, on a small sigh.

Finally…

She felt every nerve ending in her body tingle in anticipation, from her head to her toes. Heard his sharp inhalation, then felt the light touch of his warm breath caress her face as he exhaled.

Oh, the delicious press of his soft and sensuous, half open lips… as she received the single most sensual kiss of her young life–

–On her cheek?

"G'nite Sparky."

She heard the distinct, husky note in his voice, linger somewhere in her brain, as dazed, she felt her eyelids flutter up.

Just in time, to watch his receding back as he walked briskly towards his car and jumped in. The engine thrummed with tremendous power, vibrating the ground under her feet for a couple seconds before he took off.

And all without so much as a backward glance.

"Hullo?"

"Just checking that you got in, safe and sound."

"Uh…yeah. I'm good. Thanks…

"…You left in a hurry tonight… I didn't get to tell you how much I appreciated what you did…with that loser Brad I mean. And…I realize now, what I did. What I've been doing. It prob'ly wasn't fair to you. I was just so hurt by what I thought was your betrayal, which is weird, I know 'cause it's not like we were even together, or anything. I guess that's why I've been acting so crazy.

"No…wait…that's not true. I'd like to be able to blame some kinda lapse in sanity, but the truth is…I was afraid. Afraid of how I felt then…and I'm still afraid of how I feel now, I think. I don't open up easily… Trust…easily.

"Yuh know, my prayer for quite a while now was to be able to truly forgive and even forget you…uh, forget what you did. Well, what I thought you did. But as it turns out, there was nothing to forgive. And tonight, I felt such a weight lifted off me when I learned the truth. A weight I wouldn't have been carrying, *shouldn't* have been carrying, if I'd only faced my fears and confronted you earlier. We could have talked this out years ago. Had an honest conversation like we did tonight. But instead, I kept up this silly, and as it turns out, completely baseless feud. A barrier to what could have been a meaningful friendship.

"So, I guess what I'm saying is. I'm sorry for how I've been acting because now, I'm the one who needs forgiveness…from you. So, can you forgive me?"

"Absolutely. One hundred percent… Apology accepted. And thanks…for trusting me enough to share all that. It means a whole lot."

…

…

"Okay… so… friends, I guess?"

…

…

"Sure…friends."

"Well, I guess I'll see you Friday night? And thanks again for checking on me… G'nite."

"G'nite Marly…sweet dreams."

She smiled, hearing the smile in his voice,

before he rang off.

Well, as it turned out, this honesty thing wasn't too bad after all.

She smiled again, even as a mix of nervousness and blossoming excitement fought for precedence in her mind and heart.

Chapter 14

Isaiah 64:6
But we are all as an unclean thing, and all our
righteousness are as filthy rags; and we all do fade
as a leaf; and our iniquities, like the wind, have
taken us away…

Marly opened the energy shield at the back of her old apartment complex.

A mixture of trepidation and bubbling excitement fought for precedence in her mind and heart.

Well, that and straight-up disbelief.

That she'd managed to find herself back in a place in the void she'd actually visited before. Normally it was somewhere different every time. Diverse, changing faces, almost always erratic experiences, albeit all leading to her seeking the inevitable conclusion.

Urgent escape.

It was a gloomy day on this occasion, making the pool look murky gray from the outset, rather than the bright luminescent turquoise of her initial experience.

Well, no illusions this time.

Plus, she was not alone.

Anxious to get through the rough stuff so she could meet her angel and enjoy another ocean excursion, she ignored the curious looks of the dozen or so souls, clustered around the surrounding walkway, as she sprinted past them, and dove right into the chilly water.

Not even bothering to hold her breath this time, she inhaled as normal as she began treading water, just as she had before.

WHAM!

She was hit with a sudden and very icy blast of energy that tumbled her over and over, turning her watery world upside down.

"Oomph!" She felt the breath get knocked out of her as she hit solid earth.

Hard.

The normal laws of physics didn't really apply within the void. So much so, she sometimes struggled to keep her feet on the ground, to walk normally, when the powers that be seemed to want everyone and everything to float. So, unaccustomed to the feel of normal gravity pressing her down, and feeling her anxiety rise, at the unexpected turn of events, it took her a moment to reorient herself.

Pushing herself to her knees and then to her feet, she stood and took a minute to look around. It was night and she was standing on a road. Dozens of people were walking past her, or perhaps shuffling past was a better description, as she became aware of the constant, dull scraping sound of their feet echoing in the stillness. Joining their ranks in the hope of moving this leg of her journey along, she walked forward for a bit until the line slowed to a crawl and then came to a complete standstill.

Stepping out to the side, she noted their destination and started walking in that direction. Worried at first, they might notice and target her, she walked quickly but soon realized there was no danger as they all seemed entirely absorbed in themselves. As with heads bowed to a man, or woman, they kept their eyes down, focused on the ground beneath their dragging feet. As she drew nearer to the top of the line she halted, assaulted all of a sudden by an unnatural heat, and the smell of burning…

Dear God…was that sulphur?

"You should leave."

She spun at the sound of the voice echoing at the back of her brain.

It was a woman, tall, blond, striking. Easily the best-looking soul she'd ever seen, in all the time she'd been travelling. Standing a few paces back in the line.

Dressed in rags.

"Nothing grows here." She pointed to the dry and burnt, spiny-branched remnants of a tree. One of just a few that dotted the chillingly dark and barren landscape.

"It's a place of nothing but death…and regret. You don't belong here. Go, fly now, while you still

can. They'll be coming."

"What? Who?" was all she could think, still in shock over what she'd just witnessed, and that she could understand the woman so well.

"The lost souls. The fallen. The father of lies. He's always a thought away," she said the last with tangible bitterness. *"And he can't escape it, you see. This end."* She pointed towards the mouth of the smoking cavern. *"It's inevitable. Can happen at any time, so he carries it with him. They all do. Even the ones who walk the earth. The manifestation of damnation. The fire. The smell. It's never far away...from them all.*

"Either way, take your pick. They'll be on you soon enough, drawn like moths to a flame."

"But why, how?"

"It's your spark... The light of the saved. Shines out of your heart, an aura around you that's warm, and like a bright beacon in the midst of all this cold darkness. A light to rival even the brightest blessed angel."

"Come away then. Come with me." Thinking she was another living soul like her and Dani, she thought they could leave the awful wasteland together.

"Too late for me." She shook her head.

Moved in the moment, Marly did something she'd never done with a soul before. She reached out and touched her arm. But then pulled her hand back just as quickly.

Alarmed, at a degree of cold that all but burned.

"I won't become like them. Lost. The ones who wander this ghastly plane of existence, trying to

delay fate, as though they could somehow cheat the second death. It's time... Time to accept the choice I made."

"What? What choice is that?"

"Separation...from God."

Stunned, Marly felt tears spring to her eyes.

"Don't waste your tears on me. Instead, when the doubts come, the ones that lead to self-reliance, to sinful indulgence, and then to creeping pride, remember me. All the trappings of ego, the money, clothes, jewels, the status...all gone in the end. Remember...that in the end, all that's left...is you. The real you. Not the mask you wear to impress or shield yourself. To deceive, or... to hide."

Feeling that she saw her too well, Marly sensed the depth of her gaze like a physical touch. Reaching into her soul and taking her to task.

"It all gets stripped away and what's left, is the person you've become. Inside. And we are all of us, nothing but filthy, useless rags... Without Him.

"Remember this..." She pierced her again with a dark, empty, and soulless gaze, *"...and hold fast to your faith. To His love. That's all that matters. Let nothing take it from you. Ever. Now go."*

Marly nodded. Gathering a burst of speed, she took to the skies, and didn't look back.

Flying fast, she arced through the dark sky. Dismissed any thought of encountering her angel and instead prayed only to see the light. Over a black turbulent ocean, and on through a thick forest of floating trees she flew, until she saw it.

A wall.

Ahead in the distance and moving in fast.

Oh God, no...

In an instant, before she could even react, a floor rose up beneath her and a ceiling descended from above, even as the wall encircled her. Seeing no path around it she flew straight on, to just go through it. Increasing her speed, she hit it at high velocity and bounced right off. Tumbling and somersaulting in midair, she righted herself and tried again. And still, it maintained a kind of elasticity she had never before encountered. Anxious now since she was fast losing the little light left in the room, she pressed her hand against the springy surface, flew higher, pressed again, and higher still until she was stretched out, full length, against the ceiling.

Unable to see now due to the complete darkness, still she used her hands to keep feeling for any space, however small that might allow her to escape. Feeling like sticky webbing now, it clung to her hands and feet, hemming her in even further. Terrified and frantic, she felt a new chill in the room. The loud, unintelligible chatter began, as they started pressing in on her in earnest. Their stifling, chilling presence and droning calls, deafening in the stillness. Feeling her silent tears begin to flow down her cheeks despite her promise to herself to remain strong, she began humming her favorite hymn – "Great is Thy Faithfulness." Singing it loudly then, in an attempt to drown out their noise. And miracle of miracles a single voice joined her choir of one. Sounding far away at first, it got steadily louder and stronger – a rich, warm, perfect baritone, echoing around her head.

The voice of an angel.

" 🎵 *All I have needed thy hand hath provided*
Great is Thy faithfulness, Lord unto me... 🎵 "
The awful droning sound stopped abruptly, and they both let the last beautiful, lingering note of the hymn's chorus end.

Utter silence reigned, except for the sound of the powerful swishing of his wings as he approached. She smiled through her tears as finally she felt his warm, comforting presence settle at her back. And in place of the icy grip of clawing fingers, his gentle touch on her shoulder.

"So, you did all this, just so you could hear me sing? Is that it?"

She let out a little laugh, caught on a sob, as she continued to cry. Although now, in grateful relief.

"I'm here now... Please don't cry. I'm right here."

She felt his arm then, like a band of iron, encircling her waist with heartening strength, right before they blasted off amid the darkness.

Still unnerved and paralyzed by residual fear, she closed her eyes, grasped his arm at her waist with both hands, and just hung on, as he flew them at tremendous speed, way faster than they ever had before.

Up and up, they climbed, and finally, floated free. She relaxed, anticipating the arrival of the light. But then let out a shriek as all of a sudden–

She dropped.

Onto a soft, padded seat?

Her eyes snapped open, and she looked around. It was still dark though not so much that she couldn't make out her surroundings. She was sitting in a peaceful clearing, near a wooded area, in one of those Carnival ride pods, under the faint light of a watery moon.

She could smell the soft scent of fresh cut grass and wildflowers in the air around her. Could hear the melodic sound of the water in a nearby babbling brook. The chirping of frogs and the distant call of an owl off and on, as the flicker of silent candle flies lit the night air here and there.

Anxious to see what adventure lay ahead, she was about to stand so they could explore the idyllic space together. But instead, she felt the press of his hands on her shoulders, urging her to stay in her seat.

"I wouldn't do that if I were you. You're going to want to hang on, for this one."

And she did.

Gripped the soft cushion on either side of her thighs, for dear life, as the sudden force of the initial acceleration pressed her back into her seat. She heard his joyous shout behind and all around her, as they rocketed across the grass at the speed of a commercial jet ready for takeoff.

Lifting off the ground soon enough, they rose up high into the air, flying fast over top of gigantic trees, cliffs, expanses of sandy desert, then lakes, waterfalls, rivers, and vast oceans. Red-hot molten lava erupting upward from a nearby volcano, both lit and heated the night sky. Not to be outdone by the frigid temperature of the snow-capped mountains that next came into view by the light of the moon. About to protest that she wanted to linger over the many picturesque landscapes, she put a hand over one of his on her shoulder–

"Wait for it…"

She lost her breath instead, as they continued upward, piercing the clouds, then rocketing out into the stratosphere, and then finally, into space. Around the moon, on through Alpha Centauri they went, and then on, past Mars, Jupiter, Saturn, and so many billions of stars, all looking like giant balls of hot, colorful, glowing gas. Out of the Milky Way they journeyed, onto Andromeda, and across the limitless expanse of the universe.

Able to see the indescribable, awe-inspiring, and utterly humbling splendor of God's immense creation, and at such close range, was far beyond anything she could ever hope, or dream to imagine. Her heart expanded with such gratitude she could hardly contain the blissful feeling.

And this time, the light that ushered in her return to her tiny reality was her view of the earth from space, shining like a beautiful blue beacon in the sun. In perfect alignment with the other planets.

All pointing her way back home.

Chapter 15

Proverbs 6:15
Therefore, shall his calamity come suddenly;
suddenly shall he be broken without remedy...

"Yep, those two, right there, please." Marly smiled and pointed to the fresh apple and cream cheese-filled croissants she wanted. She paid the French patisserie's cashier, grasped the fragrant parcel and rushed out the door.

She'd decided to surprise Buddy with the pastries to go along with the coffee at their Friday morning meeting, so she stopped at the bakery first before hustling into her favorite corner cafe near the park.

She'd missed her morning alarm and was running a bit late – thanks to her exhilarating space odyssey, all courtesy of a certain angel, and her very own personal shuttle to the stars. She stopped herself from giggling out loud, just barely, and smiled instead as she felt the return of her pleasurable thrum.

Like Spiderman's 'spidey tingle' she imagined, she had her own faith-inspired, grace-filled vibration. Her daily reminder that God was indeed good and mighty.

Never very far away, it was fortunate, she'd discovered she could bring it back to a degree, any time she wanted, with just a little focused thought, a quiet prayer, or simple silent gratitude.

Never failing to lend a certain brightness to her day, and such deep, blessed and secret comfort to her heart.

She looked at the line. Not too bad. There were just four people ahead of her, so she pulled her glasses down from where they were perched on top of her head and started checking her social media feed in privacy mode, as she waited.

A man passed her, bumped her arm. Hard. Very nearly sending her and her precious pastries tumbling, into the person ahead of her.

"Hey! Watch it. I'm standing here!" She flicked off her AI feed and stuck her glasses back into her hair as she felt her Father God, Creator, and Spirit gifted, angel-inspired buzz evaporate. Heard a few gasps from the people around her. Male and female. Only then realizing from his towering size and their reactions, that he was probably a defender making one of those really rare public appearances. Still, she refused to back down, especially when she noticed his progress, which took him directly to the ordering counter. A brief sideways glare from him to the person at the front of the line, was all it took for that person to step aside, and back up several steps.

Oh, hell no, he didn't!

"Hey you! Culturally-bankrupt!"

He glanced back, and she heard even louder gasps.

"Yeah. I'm talking to you. Are yuh blind?!" She stepped out of the line and right up to his back as he stood at the counter. She tiptoed up and tapped him on the shoulder with her free hand as he continued to ignore her. "Or maybe, you think we don't matter in your food chain, and you're just pretending you didn't see me, and these four other people standing in line, right in front of you. Is that it?" She stepped back a few paces as he spun around.

She glared across and up at him.

His face turned purple and for a split second it contorted to the point where it no longer looked normal. He took a quick menacing step towards her, and at the same time raised and then drew back a fist. Her gasp now joined with the others around her, as she lifted her own hand, not in threat, but to protect herself.

"Hey! Unless you wanna lose the use of that hand, permanently," Newton snarled at him, "I strongly suggest you lower it and back off. Right. Now."

She hadn't even seen when he came in, but in an instant and in the nick of time, he'd stepped around in front of her. Grateful for his intervention, she welcomed his touch as he put a gentle hand to her arm and guided her even further behind him, to where she could only barely see Culturally-bankrupt's head above his. Chilled, she glimpsed his mean, beady, black eyes as he glared at her over her rescuer's shoulder.

The defender's eyes widened then, and he took a few steps back, until his big butt hit the counter behind him. She sure wished she could have seen Newton's expression right then because for the defender to stagger back like that, it must have been priceless.

"I'd do as he says, old chap. Not that I'd ever need any help dispatching the likes of you, but you know jolly well what *we'll* do to you if you don't."

She spun, at the sound of Buddy's cultured accent behind her. It had a sharp, predatory, and protective edge to it she hadn't heard from him before. As did the expression on his handsome face. And she liked it.

Former peril aside, she wasn't mad at all to be in the middle of such a very sexy, studly sandwich. She turned to the side, enjoying the tall, manly presence of both her heroes at her left and right. Resisted the childish urge to stick out her tongue at the defender, and instead, watched with added satisfaction as he hustled past them to the doorway, and disappeared into the crowd on the sidewalk.

"You, okay?" Newton turned to her. His warm, brown eyes alive with genuine concern, as he brushed a couple strands of her hair off her cheek and tucked them behind her ear.

"Oh, yeah." Thrown by the tender touch, she tried to hide her reaction with a joke, "Uh…never better, actually. Couldn't yuh tell?" She gave him a cheeky smile.

He eyed her and gave her his own quirky grin.

"Dang Sparky…"

She rolled her eyes.

"Most people would head in the opposite direction if there's even a chance they could do, or say something, to be on the receiving end of a Verndari beat-down. You got some grape nuts on you, for real. You know that?" He ran a hand through the thick waves of his hair and shook his head on a chuckle.

"Me? What about you? And stop calling me Sparky." She tried to look mad, as he smiled and winked. "The way you stood up to that guy. I mean, seriously? Did yuh see him? He was like twice your size. He coulda squashed you like a bug, Newton."

"Really?"

"Oh, my bad. That didn't come out right." She winced as she saw the expression on his face. "What I meant to say was thank you. I think my mouth wrote a cheque my butt could never cash." She grinned.

"Don't mention it. It was nothing."

"No, that was definitely not nothing. It was amazing what you did. For real." She put her free hand on his chest, felt the unexpected ripple of well-defined muscle beneath his suit.

She drew in a sharp breath, looked up, as he placed his hand over hers.

Held her breath, as their gazes collided, then lingered.

"Ahem," Buddy cleared his throat behind her.

"Oh, where are my manners." She snatched her hand back. "Dax Newton meet my dear friend Budbringer. Buddy, Dax Newton is a colleague in the media fraternity."

They shook hands, both taking each other's measure.

"Oh, so *this* is the infamous–" Buddy gave her a confused look as she shifted quickly to stand behind Dax. "No. No," she mouthed and shook her head.

"… Ah…Dax…Newton?"

She used her index finger in a slicing motion against her throat. Then flicked her hair off her shoulder and compressed her lips, as the very object of her silent discussion with Buddy, turned to look back at her.

"Infamous, huh?" His left eyebrow quirked upward, along with that side of his mouth. "You know, if I weren't such a secure man, I might start to take this really personally. Correct me if I'm wrong, but didn't we resolve all this the other night at Joe's?"

"Oh no… I mean, yeah. Of course we did. I just…uh…may have mentioned you once…uh…or…actually more times," she corrected, as she watched Buddy in his turn, mouth the words "be honest" over Newton's head.

He nodded once.

"Uh…yeah, you came up in my conversations with Buddy. When he and I were chatting. I asked his advice and yuh know, getting a man's perspective on us, or rather on our situation, was really quite useful. But then that was a while before…when we…uh–"

"You mean when we made up and I kissed you?" He gave her a lazy grin just chock full of male satisfaction.

"Ooo-we! Damn! You go, Marly-girl He's a cutie too."

She spun towards the barista behind the counter, who she knew from her nearly daily trips into the cafe. "Sshh…" she shushed them both, then lowered her voice and looked around to see who else might be listening to their conversation. "Take it easy, Jem. It was just a kiss on the cheek, okay?" She turned but then spun right back to face the counter. "And, seriously? Like shouldn't you be getting my coffee order, or something," she snapped.

"Well, I would baby-girl, if you'd placed it."

"Oh right, sorry, my bad. I'll take a plain decaf please, and a–"

"Oh no! Uh-uh, Miss Thing. I know you're not plannin' on cuttin' the line. Not when just for you and for that very reason, your…mmm…just gorgeous friends over there, were getting ready to kick that big boy's Verndari a–"

"Ah-ah…allow me!" Buddy called out as he hastily stepped over, into position at the back of the now seven-person line.

"Oh no, Buddy, I couldn't let you do that." She hustled over to him.

"Think nothing of it. Escort her out safely for me, will you?"

Right beside her, Newton nodded.

"There's a good chap." He turned back to her. "Now, why don't you go on ahead and have a bit of a chat while you wait, ay?" He gave her a pointed look. "I'll be along presently, with the coffees. Mocha-madness for you, is it?" He beamed and winked. Seeming at complete ease again. "Carry on then, off you go."

She grinned in return and nodded. Pleased he

remembered her favorite selection, she took his hint and turned to head outside.

"Good job, brothers." In his mind Gabriel went back in earth time and communicated silently with both Verge and Gyám at the moment they sent the exile packing. The two guardians briefly bumped their glowing clenched fists together and nodded. Then he watched their light recede back into their hearts as they moved to stand close beside their charges once more.

Popping back to the present he watched as they all headed out of the café. He already knew that particular outcast's days were numbered, so it didn't even signify that he'd blown his cover. There'd be no need to pursue a Legion member that would be cosmic dust within hours. If anything, Marly had actually bought the creature some time.

He hadn't been in there for coffee.

Just when she'd intercepted him, he'd thought he was heading to a meeting with one of the Legion rebels in the back of the café, the ones plotting to try to seize power from the father of lies. But what he didn't know was that the lead exile was already onto him, and he was actually headed to his end.

It was quite ironic really that the one who had staged the single most significant coup in all the world's history was himself under constant siege, having to continually surveil his disloyal followers.

From the very beginning of the fall, discord had always been bubbling right under the surface.

But since news of Andeo's demise at Alrissa's office, his repentance, and his subsequent return to the welcoming embrace of the Creator spread like wildfire, knowledge of the true depth of the chief liar's deception had stirred up an unprecedented degree of bitterness and rage in the rest of the fallen. So much so that their leader was having to thwart numerous, simultaneous, and persistent uprisings, across multiple dimensions.

Poetic justice indeed, that all in God's good timing, the evil one's entire operation on earth would collapse, and essentially implode. Dismantled. From the inside out.

It was just left to him and his brothers to help save as many of God's beloved children as would so choose in the interim.

Standing in the queue in Marly's place, he decided on exactly how he'd let her know that while he was grateful for her kind offer, he wouldn't be consuming the pastry she'd bought to surprise him. Carefully, and with tact, naturally, so he wouldn't hurt her feelings. Much like Michael and his choice of club soda, he barely tolerated the decaf coffee for appearances, but that was where he drew the line. Once one had tasted the joys of heaven in communion with the Three in One everything else was…well…less than nothing.

He centered himself in His will. Popped back and forth into the minds of the people around him. Leaving a feeling of wellbeing here, erasing a negative thought there. Helped that young man to recall just the right verse of scripture to meditate on, given what was about to befall him. Urged the young woman behind him to remember to repeat her positive affirmation – that she did indeed matter, despite how she was being taken for granted by her family. And back to Marly. To whom he gave his most potent blessing. For a life filled with love, continuing devotion to God, marital harmony, strength to endure, and at the appropriate times, just the right number of moments…

Of utter delight!

Watching her step out onto the street, he continued to commune with his Creator in quiet adoration.

Chapter 16

2 Corinthians 5:17
Therefore, if any man be in Christ, he is a new
creature: old things are passed away; behold, all
things are become new…

Newton waved a hand over the sensor near the café door and allowed her to step out onto the street in front of him.

"*Just,* a kiss on the cheek? I have to say, that one really hurt, Sparky. That was some of my best work the other night."

"Really?" She rolled her eyes. "And again, with the Sparky."

He chuckled.

"So, "dear friends", huh? Since when are you so friendly with a defender?"

"What makes you think he's a defender?" She shrugged and got set to obfuscate or bluff her way out if necessary.

"Seriously?"

"What?"

"We're really doing this, right now?"

She eyed him.

"I'm a journalist, Marly, and contrary to your opinion, a very good one. And what you may not know is, I don't just make a great living off it, I'm *all* about it. I have an unquenchable thirst for knowledge. I literally thrive on being curious, detail-oriented, and ultra-observant, *and* I don't stop… Ever. Till I get my story."

She set her expression to blank.

"Okay, I see…so it's like that." He shook his head on a smile.

"Let's see… First off, the obvious – defenders have only one name, and you introduced him as Budbringer. Now, you're a full name kinda girl. So, if he was human, I'm pretty sure you would have told me his first name too.

"Then there's the look. His eye color is that unique, striking blue of all the ones the defenders set before the human public as liaisons. The face of their species if you will. Probably intentional, to put men at ease, and impress the ladies. Because God knows, that soulless black the rest of them have, it's just downright creepy. Also undeniable is his build. Verndari make 'em big. It's really hard to miss that kind of height, bulk, bone structure, and musculature.

"Next, to the untrained ear, his accent would suggest he's British, but I minored in linguistics, so *I* know he's not. See, he speaks like the Royals, or the peerage. The issue with that is, since the turn of the century, all male British nobility, to a man, from baron on up to duke, they're all fiercely loyal to their own brand. The entire world came together once the defenders arrived, so it's one of the few ways they can continue to set themselves apart. So now, they wouldn't be caught dead in anything that didn't come straight out of Savile Row. Your friend, however, is wearing a monogrammed suit right off the runway. The Armani's Spring Collection runway. This year's. And I know that because I've got one just like it sitting in my closet at home. So, speaking English with a crisp, British upper crust accent, without actually being British nobility? Now that, is just textbook Verndari.

"Last, there isn't a rational human being on the planet who thinks they can take on a defender on their own, and win, but your new friend there sounded really confident he wouldn't need any help with that. Only defenders take on defenders. So, that makes him either dumb as a box of rocks, certifiably insane, or, one of them. I don't know about you, but he didn't sound stupid, *or* crazy to me. Plus, the intonation in his voice when he told the line-cutter he should know what *"we'll* do to him," if he didn't step off." Well, that tells me he was talking about somebody, or bodies, associated with him either personally, or professionally. Bodies, I might add, who could pose a real and formidable threat to the guy. The only beings on the planet who fall into that category are, again, other Verndari.

"Besides, much as I'd like to flatter myself, he never even glanced in my direction when he said "we", so, suffice it to say, when he said it, he for sure wasn't talkin' about him and me.

"So, we're back to my original question – since when…are you friends with a defender, Sparky?"

Okay…

WOW…

AND a happy cow.

She jammed her free hand into her jacket pocket and then compressed her lips just in case she gave in to her really strong desire to break into spontaneous applause, right then. And to prevent her mouth from falling open to gape at him in sheer shock and awe. Forget being an ace reporter, with that little performance, he should have def joined the NYPD and become a detective like Dani!

Of course she'd never admit it to him, but he'd just impressed the heck out of her with that little Sherlock Holmes display of deductive reasoning. Aside from being just plain awesome, it was sexy as hell.

In truth, she was more than a little turned on right then.

She took in a calming and centering breath. Considered and strategized her next move like they were engaged in the World Chess Championship.

"And speaking of not being crazy or stupid. Neither are you. *And* you're not a defender. If your little theory holds true, what's your excuse? You just took on one of them on your own and thought you could win."

"Who said I thought I could win? Plus, I just haven't shown you my…uh…particular brand of crazy... Yet…"

He gave her a look.

One that would have made her sweat, in the dead of winter.

Oh…he's good… No doubt.

Plus, her 'OMG, he's so hot right now' meter jumped right up, a few dozen more notches, at least.

She dug deep. Racked her brain. 'Cause this last one, was for all the marbles.

"So, you studied Linguistics in college, huh?"

He nodded, even as a slight smile lifted his lips.

"Really? How many languages can you speak?"

"Excluding English, eight fluently and some others…enough to get by."

"You?!" She snorted. "You're kidding me, right?"

"Not even a little bit."

"Prove it."

"Let's see… Pas même un peu. Ni siquiera un poquito. Nemmeno un po'. Nicht einmal ein bisschen…"

…Russian, Mandarin, Hindi, Egyptian Arabic – he rattled off the eight, with ease. One by one. Plus, Portuguese, Japanese, Urdu, Farsi and a couple others she didn't even recognize in his mini, round the world, language trip.

So, aside from being a strong, honest-to-goodness, decent, man of God…

*He's good-looking, crazy-sexy-smart, **and** he speaks fluent French too?*

Dang…

The thirst trap trifecta…

She caught herself, before she moaned out loud.

Didn't matter though 'cause she was still unsure he was the one for her… Right?

"…Yuh neva know say, nuh even a likkle?" His head tilted to the side, his left brow popped up, as he finished the tour.

"Wait…was that last one some kinda West Indian patois?"

"Jamaican, actually."

"Okay, so now you're *seriously* just showing off."

"Not really. Not sure I even said it right…" He said something under his breath she didn't catch.

"Sorry? What was that?"

"I said I just picked it up. While I was on vacation in Montego Bay last year."

He chuckled, as she giggled.

"Wow, well, it's never a dull moment with you, huh Newton?"

He shrugged as his laughter faded. And she finally…gracefully, and perhaps gratefully, accepted her defeat at the hands of an exceptional and formidable opponent.

"Okay look, you're right about Buddy. A mutual friend introduced us. He's been helping me with…uh…a story. He's nothing like the others by the way. He's…different."

"I'll bet."

"What? What was that? If I didn't know better, I'd say you were jealous. Seriously? You are, aren't you?" She grinned as she noticed his expression and the tightness along his jawline.

And secretly, she reveled in it.

God knew, it had taken them four long years to get here, but it finally felt like they were both on the same page, at the same time, and headed in the same direction – forward.

Together.

It felt old. Dependable. Like a comfortable pair of well-worn shoes. Yet, brand new. And exciting. All at the same time.

And absolutely awesome!

"Well, if you must know, it's strictly professional. Well mostly. Except for the times he gave me some personal advice, like I said before, but he was really more like a father figure when he did that."

"Okay, if you say so."

He still didn't look fully persuaded, so she got set to convince and distract him.

"So, they must be paying you pretty good at Earth Network, if you can afford off the runway Armani, huh? I'll bet it looks really good on you too." She reached out and placed her free hand on his chest as she'd done inside the café, minutes earlier.

He looked down at her hand and then into her eyes.

She let her lips curve into a slight smile. Drew his gaze right to them, as she moistened just one side of her bottom lip, with the gentle scrape of her teeth.

"Yeah…uh…like they say, it's only money, right?" He cleared his throat.

Check…

"Plus… I'm guessing *you'd* know a little something about that yourself." His brows popped up for a second, his head tilting to the side as he grasped her fingers at his chest and without breaking eye contact, raised them to his lips.

He placed a soft and sensual kiss on her

knuckles.

As she watched.

"Huh?"

Mesmerized alternately by the depths of his beautiful bronze gaze, and by the delicious sight and sensation of his mouth… His soft. Perfect. Half-open lips…pressing against her skin. She lost all thought.

"These, I mean." He released his hold on her hand and tapped the edge of the frame of her glasses resting atop her head. "Bet these Televisios set you back quite a bit. Am I right?" Just the very tip of his tongue ran the gamut between his lips. From one end to the other, for just a second. Then he sent her his own slow, ultra, alpha-male smile.

And just like that, the game's afoot, yet again.

"Ah…touché, Sherlock. Well…played, indeed." It was her turn to clear her throat as her words came out low and husky.

Checkmate…

A giggle bubbled up in her then, to match his deep chuckle, even as she resisted the sudden urge to fan herself.

Turning away for a moment, she looked up and down the busy sidewalk, instead.

"Wow, I still cannot believe that guy. First, he bumps me like I don't even matter, then when I saw him cutting the line…ooo… I just lost it, yuh know? I mean the nerve." She got annoyed all over again as she recalled it.

"There's actually this 'truther' I've been following. He's amazing! He's on all the major social feeds. Calls himself Digital Dante 'cause he's a real big fan of the ultra-classical writer, from the early thirteen hundreds. You know his poems?”

He nodded slowly as a half-smile crept along his lips.

“What?”

“Nothing. Go on.”

“So anyway, just the other day, he sent me this really cool quote that just resonated with me. It suggested the darkest places in hell are reserved for those who maintain their neutrality, in times of moral crisis. I think that’s the gist of it. Anyway, when that guy came in, I just kept thinking, defender or not, what he was doing was just so wrong, and if no one spoke up, well…he’d just think he could get away with it. Do it again, or maybe something even worse next time. I just didn’t want that on my conscience.

“Plus, I tell you what,” she put a hand on his arm, “if there’s even a scintilla of truth and accuracy to that assertion, aside from trusting in my Lord and Savior, I have no intention of doing anything that could cause me to spend a single second, far less an eternity of my afterlife, in any hellish space.”

He gave a low chuckle. “Funny you should mention Dante.”

He put a hand over hers on his arm. After already enjoying the arousing press of his lips there, she felt the light caress like a jolt of electricity as his fingers brushed back and forth across hers.

“You’re not gonna believe this, but–”

“Right. One mocha-madness for the lovely and incredibly gutsy lady.”

She spun for the second time that morning at the sound of Buddy’s voice. He held out her coffee.

“Thanks Buddy. How’d you get this so quick?”

She accepted the trendy, insulated coffee-drink canister. "Not counting the ones, you were standing behind who came in after, there were at least four other people ahead of me when Culturally-bankrupt came in like he owned the place."

"Culturally-bankrupt?" Both men spoke at the same time, looked at each other, and then at her.

They burst out laughing.

"Oh, now that's just brilliant, that is." Buddy put a hand to her shoulder and continued laughing. "Did he hear you call him that?"

She nodded.

"Well, no wonder that blighter got as angry as he did."

"Yeah, that's a classic, for real."

"Yeah, it actually was kinda clever, if I do say so myself." She grinned. "So, Buddy, you were telling me, did he scare off the people ahead of me in line, or what?"

"Oh, no," his laughter died off, "they were discussing what happened amongst themselves. Even with the couple people who came in after the fact. They all admired your fortitude in speaking up. Good for you! They even thought that what I did for you was so chivalrous, they insisted that I go to the head of the queue, on the spot. I'll tell you what. Gives me renewed faith in human nature. It truly does." He got a wistful look on his face for just a moment. "Well, shall we crack on then, Ms. Sparks? I expect you've got to get to your newsroom, and we still haven't had our little chat. Here, allow me to carry that for you." He relieved her of the pastry bag.

"Oh yeah…uh, of course," she looked over at

Dax, "I'll catch up with you later? Tonight? At Dani and Joe's?"

"Oh, yeah sure," he nodded. "It's a date."

"Cool."

She looked back after she and Buddy had moved away.

Smiled and raised a hand in farewell as she noted him still standing. Unchanged. Seemingly following her progress as she walked away.

"So, a date, is it? Well, that sounded rather promising. Your little tète-a-tète went even better than expected, I take it?"

"Yeah, yeah…don't get too excited though. We'll see." She turned back, rolled her eyes at him, as he beamed.

"Oh, and thanks again for standing up for me back there." She glanced at him as they headed for their park bench. "What are the odds? I can't believe you came in just then. Wait, just a minute." She stopped walking and grasped his arm to halt his advance. "I'll bet this is another of those just assume you can find me anywhere at any time kinda deals, isn't it?"

"And I…will not confirm or deny any of that, Ms. Sparks." He gave her a winning smile.

"You know, we've shared a whole lot together Buddy, you can call me Marly, yuh know."

"I could, but then that just wouldn't be us. Now, would it?"

She considered his words, realizing he was right. Somehow, just like their unique, special and indispensable dynamic, his formal address for her just seemed to fit.

He grasped her fingers and placed them in the crook of his elbow as he started them walking again. "Come along, Ms. Sparks, I dare say, your remarkable destiny awaits."

Chapter 17

Proverbs 16:9
A man's heart deviseth his way: but the LORD
directeth his steps...

My fellow skeptical Americans...
Don't look now, but a new destiny awaits.
It's really happening. As I write this, marches
are being organized in protest of the Defender
Agenda. Not just here in states all across the country,
but also around the globe, as more and more people
have been waking up and demanding answers to the
questions we've been asking in this space for months.
And not a minute too soon because today's
footage is guaranteed to blow your mind.
As if we didn't have enough to worry about
with the secret weapons tests, and the floor to ceiling
portal to Hades in the basement of the Verndari
diplomatic Center, internal sources have captured a
defender changing, morphing. Transforming into a
human being is prob'ly the best description for what
you're about to see.
Yes, you heard me right. They can apparently
change into any one of us, at any time. Wonder why

they neglected to mention that little talent? Just imagine the level of deception it takes to conceal something like that for 25 years! It's just staggering.

And they won't be able to bury this one before it hits mainstream media. This story is way too big, too important. Hell, not even their obscene amounts of ill-gotten gains will buy them out of this one.

So, still think they're the saviors of the world? If you do, you might want to wake up real quick and get on the right side of this fight because make no mistake, a conflict is beginning, and every single person on this planet is going to have to choose which side they're on.

You decide.

Till next time, anxious to hear from you.

Cynical in NYC

"Saw your last post." Dani dropped her voice and pulled her to the side in the foyer while the others were talking at the door. "And there's even more I can tell you. You found out about the shapeshifting, but that isn't the half of it. Have you ever heard of hosting?"

"Is that…what it sounds like? Like them taking over a human body?"

"Yep. And I'm not talking about a *Star Trek - Deep Space Nine* warm and fuzzy Trill, volunteering to share their body with some wise and friendly thousand-year-old symbiont, type situation. We're talking *Stargate* type aliens. Remember when we watched that series?" She glanced to the door. "I mean like full-on, nasty, freakin' Gao'uld. Frying your brain. Systematically and totally taking you over and causing the end of all life as you know it kinda thing." She took in a deep breath.

"Okay, so that was a mouthful."

"You're telling me. Saw it firsthand, with my very own eyes."

"What? You're kidding me, right?"

"I wish I was. For a couple months now, Duncan and I have been quietly working on different leads we've been getting from Svikari. And believe me, *girl*, we have seen some freaky stuff. Call me tomorrow?"

"Yeah…of course."

They hugged.

To say she was intrigued and more than a little weirded out was putting it mildly.

They all huddled, Dax said a little prayer of thanksgiving and for their continued safety and well-being, before their goodbyes at the door. Then Joe opened it and stood back so his guests could head out. Rissa and Duncan walked on ahead, hand in hand, but after initially following them, she hung back a bit and turned, just in time to see Joe and Dani saying something to Dax in the foyer.

Joe slapped him on the back, then gripped his shoulder, while Dani's chin jerked in the direction of the open doorway, while she gave him a very pointed look.

The only way they could be any more obvious was if they put up a big ol', golden, flashing neon arrow, pointing from him straight out to where she was standing.

"Okay, g'nite, you guys, and thanks again for

dinner. It was just amazing, as usual!" She called out and almost laughed as three pairs of eyes widened at once, as they all turned in her direction.

Dax hastened out and started down the front steps, while Dani and Joe waved. Both grinning like idiots, as she walked backwards and watched their front door finally slide closed.

Mischief on her mind, she decided to make him sweat just a little bit more. So, she made a sudden about face and walked at pace, across the massive, covered deck, where they'd been seated for dinner, outside. Around the picnic tables and comfy chairs, and the large outdoor island complete with sink, chiller, grill, and fryer. And last, past the exquisite collection of expensive crockery, silverware, and glassware her friends kept for entertaining. All neatly stored in a semi-circle, in a perfect blending of decorative antique wooden and glass shelving.

She'd almost made it to the other side too, before he finally caught up with her.

"Uh…Marly, wait up!"

She felt the urgent touch of his fingers grasping the back of her arm.

She smiled.

Stopped.

Right over the outer edge of the luminous platform.

She waved to Rissa and Duncan as they briefly looked back and grinned too, before practically sprinting to, and then disappearing on the incline curving down towards the driveway.

Had they all been in on some kind of 'get Dax and Marly together' covert op? Clearly, she was late to the party.

"Can I just have a word with you, before you go?"

She smiled and took her time as she turned around.

"Oh, yeah, sure. What about?"

She looked down for a moment enjoying the phenomenal view. No matter how many times she visited this home, she continued to be fascinated by the very unusual salt and freshwater feature as it sparkled with light, illuminating the assortment of marine life swimming right under her feet. Each variety in their own little habitat, sustained by numerous impenetrable energy shields.

A lobster crept by just then, along the sandy bottom of a corralled area, a fair distance down.

Enjoy your reprieve while you can, little buddy...

She was pretty sure she'd almost had him for dinner that night. She'd switched from lobster to crab at the last minute, after Joe asked them to each choose whatever seafood they wanted him to prepare especially for their nighttime feast.

"I've been meaning to tell you something, ever since we met in the café this morning. Well, even before that, actually. I have a confession to make. But I'm not sure how you're gonna take it when I tell you."

Confession?

Well, that was an odd way to broach a 'let's start a committed relationship' conversation. Still, he was unpredictable. One of the many intriguing reasons why she was so taken with him.

"Well, go on. Just spit it out, Sherlock, we're not getting any younger here."

She stooped down to hide her smile. Bounced on the balls of her feet, and tapped the surface energy shield making it buzz with brief light and power, as a curious, pretty little silver and red fish about the size of her fingernail swam by, then popped its head up near the surface.

"Okay. Yeah, sure. I guess the direct approach is best, so here goes nothing… Remember when you told me about the truther you're following who loves the works of Dante? Well, *I* am Dante. And Dante is me. There I said it. Whew," he blew out a loud breath.

"What?"

Playful pretense aborted; she rose to her feet.

"The truther you've been texting with. Digital Dante? It's me."

She made a rude noise. "No way!"

"Oh, yes way. Okay, let me see, umm… I was planning to text you tonight, with a new quote, after we'd talked. I was going to say that Dante wrote – "In that book which is my memory…on the first page that is the chapter when I first met you the words… here begins a new life." Because I guess what I'm really trying to say is, that aside from how it mirrors what I thought when I met you initially four years ago, I'd really like us to start over. Now. And have a *real,* committed relationship." He reached down and grasped her fingers, then ran his warm palms up her bare arms. "So, what do you say, *Ms. Cynic?*" He looked down into her eyes and aside from his undeniable use of Dante's pet name for her, she saw the truth of his words shining there.

"Oh, wow. It is you."

Now all the unconscious parallels she'd been drawing in her mind up until then all made sense. She should have been angered by his deception, but actually she was relieved, only just acknowledging to herself, she'd wanted it to be him. Maybe even before she'd had that soul-searching, eye-opening convo with Buddy about it. Now, to learn he was her solid anchor, her most generous and avid supporter in their cause against the defenders. Her brilliant, strong, thoughtful, brave, crazy-sexy-French-speaking, principled man of God.

Her Dante *and* her Dax. All rolled into one. Not only was she not angry…

She was thrilled!

"Okay, so I realize you may be mad I didn't tell you before but just hear me out. I had good reason, I promise. Because of our history I feel like we really needed a fresh start and a chance to be us again, as we were at G and R. Well, before us… uh…after. You know what I mean. Anyway, all of that to say, I don't care what it takes, but we are going to face this head on, talk it out, and get through whatever issues we have together. No more walking away. So go ahead cry, kick up a fuss, or go gangster, and break some stuff up in here if you need to." He waved a hand back towards their friends' wood and glass showcase.

"Seriously?" She gave him her most incredulous look.

"Yeah, exactly. Go on ahead. Have at it! None

of that stuff is mine. I don't give a bad-devil-damn!"

She looked up at him. Stunned for a moment…

Until they both burst out laughing.

"Are you kidding me right now?! I cannot believe you said that. If Dani and Joe heard that, odds are you'd be dodging bullets and knives right about now. Oh, that was just too funny!" She gave his arm a playful swat as they howled.

"So, does this mean I'm forgiven?" His laughter faded to a warm smile.

He looked down.

And so did she.

Mildly surprised, as she followed his gaze to their joined hands. Not even realizing that after swatting him she'd slid her hand down his arm and laced their fingers in a loose grasp.

It felt so familiar and comfortable, something sparked in the back of her mind. Something warm and wonderful.

"Yeah, I guess it kinda does, doesn't it?"

She swung their hands back and forth between them as they shared a little smile.

"Oh, and I wasn't even mad by the way. So sorry you wasted a perfectly good reconciliation speech for nothing."

"No worries. It's not like I missed a deadline to get Joe's advice, then rehearsed it all the way over here in the car, or anything."

She eyed him.

He shrugged.

She erupted into giggles all over again, as he chuckled.

"Come on, let me walk you out to your car." He

gave her fingers a gentle tug.

A light rain started coming down by the time they left the covered section of the deck and started walking with their fingers still entwined, along the open-air lanai.

"Here, let's go this way. Just past the pool there's another little gate that's a shorter distance out to the cars." He pointed to the right.

"Okay, lead the way."

They sprinted over and made it halfway around the pool when she slipped in her heels. Crying out, as she lost her footing. Dax turned, grabbed her and managed to steady her at the very edge of the pool. But then lost his own balance, as arms flailing, he fell backward into the water.

"Oh my gosh, Newton, you should have seen the look on your face." She giggled and pointed as he quickly resurfaced and shook his hair and the water out of his eyes.

"Yeah, yeah. Go ahead and laugh it up. Here I was, trying to save you, and that's how you do me? I guess no good deed goes unpunished, for real."

"Here, let me help you up."

Still laughing, she grasped his right hand in a firm grip and took a bit of his weight as he pulled himself up and back onto the decorative cobble stone walkway that surrounded the three closed sides of the infinity pool.

Still holding onto his warm, firm hand, she looked up into his eyes.

And froze.

Chapter 18

Matthew 18:20
For where two or three are gathered together in my
name, there am I in the midst of them…

"You?!"

No, it couldn't be…

That was what felt so familiar.

She'd know that warm, firm, and strong grasp
anywhere. That sure and reassuring grip. Had felt it
on nearly every occasion she'd been in peril for the
last three months. She ran her thumb over his once
again and felt that little callous. The same one she'd
felt on her angel's hand so many times in the recent
past. And it could mean only one of two things.
Either he had the very same rough spot, in exactly the
same place, or it hadn't been her angel with her all
those times

It had been him.

All the intensely terrifying and equally powerful, exhilarating, joy-filled experiences flashed through her mind.

All except one.

She fought but couldn't recall feeling any rough spot the very first time she'd danced with her angel on that fateful day. Of course not. How stupid could she be? God's angels were obviously flawless, perfectly designed by the Creator. They'd certainly bear no human blemish, or bruise. She couldn't believe she hadn't considered that simple fact. Until now.

Still unwilling to believe her sense of touch, she held onto his hand, looked up into his eyes, now filled with what? …Concern? Apprehension?

And another emotion she wasn't sure she was ready to recognize, far less hope for.

She looked down again. Turned his hand over so she could take a closer look at his thumb, and sure enough, there was the oval shaped rough spot right near his wrist. Inspecting it closeup and in the light now, it looked like the scarring from a burn to her. And, she'd seen it before she recalled. That first night they'd both had dinner at Dani and Joe's place. She'd thought it an unusual birth mark when he held his hand to his heart and said he didn't realize she cared enough to tell Dani about him.

"First, you tell me you're Dante and now… you're the one? All those nights? You?!"

"Me." He gave a sheepish smile and shrugged.

"But how? How were you even there with me every time in the void? And after? I never saw you. Wait… But you… You recognized me, didn't you?"

She felt lightheaded.

He nodded slowly.

Realizing she was still gripping his hand she dropped it like it burned her.

"All that time and you didn't tell me? And then the Dante thing. What was it? Just all some kind of sick joke to you?!"

She stepped back, crossed her arms over her chest feeling chilled, nauseous, and short of breath, all at the same time.

Oh, dear God no, this can't be happening... not again...

"No. God no! You have to believe me." He tried to reach out for her, and she backed up even further.

"I've wanted to get close to you for so long. Then from the time we met at dinner that first night, and I found out you'd told Dani about me, everything changed. We'd barely even spoken in four years, yet you'd followed my career? I knew there had to be a chance for us still. After that I tried to create some opportunities for us to meet under casual circumstances, in real life. Like getting Joe and Dani to invite us over for dinner more often and turning up at the café you go to nearly every morning. And...and your favorite restaurant at lunch."

"Oh, my gosh, I wondered why you kept popping up all the time. Kept thinking it was fate or something. You planned that?"

"Oh yeah, to a T. Worried the entire time you'd think I was a stalker, or worse. Then Dani told me about your underground persona as 'Cynical in NYC'. She thought it might be another good way for us to connect and start from scratch without the uh…baggage, that came along with our prior interactions."

"So, us linking online, that was Dani's idea?"

"Well, aside from my personal ambition to get us closer, as soon as I saw the content you created for the Defender Agenda I was on board with the cause, for sure. But yeah, I guess it was Dani initially. Once I told her what I really wanted was for you and me to reconnect, she promised to help me. She said she'd tried to find out about your beef with me, but you weren't ready to talk about it. So, according to her, it was going to have to be a strategic battle plan, to have me attack and break down your unknown misgivings about me from two sides. Digitally anonymous one way, and in person in another, over some good food and conversation at her house. That was just a win-win as far as I was concerned. I'd get to be near you *and* eat Joe's restaurant quality meals on a regular. Trust me, she didn't have to ask me twice." He grinned. "Got a little crazy for a while there though. I almost got jealous of myself a couple times, when it was clear you liked Dante better." He shook his head on a dry chuckle.

"And our encounters in the void?"

"From that first night, we danced. I wanted so much to find a way to tell you it was me, but I just kept putting it off. Waiting for the right time. I was actually planning to tell you tonight. But before that, you were always so angry with me. I was afraid once you knew, you wouldn't want to see me there anymore, and I'd stop feeling your lure."

"My what-now?"

"I dunno what else to call it, can't explain it

myself. I just know one minute I'd be out flying, or on a random street, or in one of those freaky rooms, and the next I'd just feel this strong tug and in a second, I'd see you… Get pulled, right to you," he took a couple hesitant steps forward and peered down, into her eyes, "and I'd *be,* with you… Wherever you were, and these days, somewhere I could tell you're in grave danger, and in need of rescue. It actually started years ago when I first met you, but then it was just sporadic, and you weren't in the kind of peril I've seen you in lately."

"But you never said anything."

"Come on now, Marly, how could I? After we had our falling out, we weren't exactly friends back then, were we? I didn't even know if I could talk to you in the void given how hard it is to communicate. And I sure as hell wasn't going to walk up to you in the office and say anything. You'd have prob'ly called the nearest psych ward to have me committed." His mouth twisted upward in wry humor.

Well, she couldn't argue with that.

"But wait, how do you have wings when you're in the void?"

"Wings?"

"Yeah, I can fly but I've never had wings like yours. How do you get them?"

"Uh… I've never had wings. I just fly. Just like you do. I think."

"But that's not possible. I saw…"

Snippets of their experiences together flashed through her mind. She hadn't even seen him since he'd been behind her most of the time, and in the dark for the rest. So, if it was him the entire time…had her angel been somewhere nearby then…? She realized that while she thought she'd felt them, sensed their energy and vibration, or heard the movement of wings, she'd never actually seen them on any of those occasions.

"But then how did you even save me? All those times I was surrounded. I prayed, I fought and still I couldn't free myself, so how did you?"

"Well, that one's easy. That wasn't me."

"Huh?"

He stilled and looked right into her eyes for a long moment, and when he finally spoke, his voice was soft yet deep, and filled with Godly power…

"For where two or three are gathered together in my name, there am I…in the midst of them…"

She lost her breath.

Tears filled her eyes as she acknowledged the simple truth of his words. She experienced joy, peace, and such deep gratitude for their Creator all at once, and to such a degree, that it was very nearly overwhelming. She reached out, and they held hands for a moment, she knew, in silent, reverent prayer and thanksgiving.

"I know 'wow' doesn't even begin to cut it in this moment, but wow." Her voice got solemn and quiet. "Have you ever seen Him?"

"Yeah, I think I have, once or twice. But mostly He's like this really warm and powerful presence in the room, know what I mean? There's nothing to compare to that feeling. It's singular. You just know it must be Him."

"Yeah, I think I've felt that too. I think I saw

Him, once, a year ago. I'd had a really horrific travelling night. I kept trying to shake myself awake, but I guess I was so tired I just kept slipping from the void, back into consciousness and then back into the void again. Then while I was in the middle of an attack I prayed and begged Him to send like a battalion of holy angels to stand around me, to keep me safe from the evil invading my dreams.

"I must have fallen asleep then because the next thing I knew I woke up and it was morning, and for just a couple seconds before I opened my eyes, I saw Him. He was wearing white robes, he was bearded, and his hair was down to his shoulders all beautiful and wavy. He was sitting in a wooden chair right in front of a door straight ahead of me, but he wasn't facing in my direction. He was smiling, and I could see his mouth moving like he was talking to someone further to the right and outside of my view. He just looked so casual and comfortable; his right knee was up, his foot resting on a rung of the chair. It was just a flash, but I just knew he'd been there. All night, till I woke up. I think he wanted me to know that when I needed Him and I called, he wouldn't send anyone. He'd come Himself."

"Now that's a wow moment, for real. That. Is truly amazing."

"Yeah. It really is," she beamed. "And speaking of which, what about after the danger passed? That fabulous ride we had on the hover board out on the ocean, and that time on that shuttle that took us to the stars? I didn't think it was possible to feel that much joy in the void. Every single time I've had even a moderately pleasant experience it was short-lived and followed by something far more intense and horrific by comparison."

"Your guess may be better than mine on that one." He shook his head with a wry smile.

"So that wasn't you doing those incredible things either?"

"Oh, those were me, all right. I just mean I really don't know how I could do it. I think maybe we weren't in the void at those times. I think there's some kind of intersection between the nightmares of the void and our real dreams. So, once we get out, we automatically slide right back into them. And as for me, when I'm having a dream, most times I can control what happens next."

She shot him an incredulous look, and he shrugged. "I'm serious. Ever since I was a kid, I could basically manipulate everything around me. Fill a room with my favorite toys. Jump onto a horse and make it fly. I always thought I had a really active imagination, but then as I got older, I realized that it was actually a blessing, a kind of relief from the stresses of real life. Got me through and kept me sane after some terrifying trips into the void too, like you would not believe."

"Oh, I think I would. I saw the only other live person I think I've ever seen, who's like us. Just skewered…like some kinda freaky, spiral shish kebab, resting on this…just a gigantic, barbeque pit. Had to help pull all the metal out."

"Wow." His eyes got wide. "You mean like with the fire and everything?"

"Oh, no." She gave a vigorous shake of her head. "But I didn't know if that's what was gonna happen next. It was someone I'd never seen before at that time. But I had this strong calling to help. I was scared out of my mind, but I just knew I had to do something. Oh wow… that must be the same lure-thing you get with me."

"Exactly."

"I'm glad I heeded that call and the ones that came after too. They quite literally changed my life."

"Yeah. They can do that."

"Bless God," they both said and shared a smile.

"I still can't believe I thought you were…uh…someone else though, that first time we met, and we danced."

"Oh, yeah? Who?"

"An angel," she muttered under her breath.

"I'm sorry…come again?"

"I thought you were an angel, okay? I danced with one, once."

"Seriously?" He barked out a laugh.

"I kid you not. I really saw him and a couple others too."

"Oh, I believe you saw an angel. Hell, I figure that's just par for the course given the things we've seen." He shook his head. "It's just I couldn't even get you to dance at the office Christmas party, so I figured you didn't like dancing. Before that first night we met in the void, I sure couldn't picture you being so free and uninhibited as to dance in the air with anybody, let alone an angel."

"Well, I did, and as it happens, I love dancing. I just didn't wanna dance with you…uh, before." She snorted.

"Great! Thanks. Good to know." He flashed her

a   fake   smile.
"But, if you knew we'd never even danced before. Why'd you say "again?" when I asked you to dance, then?"

"I thought I'd misheard you, so I was just repeating the word you used because I couldn't figure out why *you* said it."

"Oh, now I get it! And I thought my angel was amused that I wanted to dance *yet* again."

"Perception," they both said at the same time. "Jinx!"

They grinned, then he just looked at her, in silence, for a few long moments, his face a picture of so many emotions.

"Well, it's getting kinda cold out." He shivered, loosened his tie and squeezed some pool water out of the end of it with a wry laugh. "I really need to get out of these wet clothes." He eyed her.

"Yeah, sure hope that's not one of your Armani off the runway numbers cause *that*… it is gonna be a bug-with-an-itch to clean. For real."

"Bug-with-an-itch? Really?" He grinned and shook his head.

She giggled.

"Sounds super cute coming from you. I like that…

"Oh, and it's ruined. No doubt." He lifted the ends of the jacket. "I can feel it shrinking on me as we speak."

Smiling, she looked around and up, realizing that while they'd been standing there the rain stopped. The clouds had dissipated, leaving a gorgeous view of a starlit sky above them.

"Yeah, well I guess I should be getting home too."

"Or…" he reached for her hand, "you could come watch an old movie at my place… Come on, it's not even that late, plus it's Friday night. I'm not working tomorrow. Are you?"

She shook her head.

"Great. So, we can stay up late. Enjoy the movie. Maybe have some popcorn and sodas? Talk some more? You like milk duds, right?" His smile was adorable.

"Are you kidding me? Who doesn't? Absolutely." She nodded and grinned. "Sure, I'd like that."

No more playing it cool tonight.

She reached for their joined hands with her free one. Held his between both of hers. "Actually… I'd like it… a whole lot."

They shared a warm look and an even warmer smile.

Take that Buddy. How's that for honesty?

Keeping a tight hold on his hand, she let him lead her out to their cars.

Chapter 19

Matthew 6:33
But seek ye first the kingdom of God, and His righteousness; and all these things shall be added unto you…

He sent her the coordinates for his home, she uploaded them to her car's auto-driver to lead her there and jumped into the back seat for the ride.

As soon as they were on their way, her car's call alert sounded.

"Hullo?"

"Guess who?"

She smiled as she heard his deep, smooth and cultured tone fill all the empty space in her car.

"Hmm…yuh know, yuh sound kinda familiar. Do I know you? Newton, is it? Or should I say Dante? Or wait, what's shakin' Sherlock?" She laughed and clapped her hands together.

"Okay, so you know it's like way too soon for me to find *any* of that, even remotely funny, right?"

"Yeah, I figured, but I just couldn't resist. You have to admit the "guess who?" was just the perfect set up for it, right?" She giggled.

"Yeah, right. *Guess...* I walked straight into that one."

"HA! Good one!"

She grinned as he chuckled.

"So, how long till we get to your place?"

"Oh, about half hour, traffic permitting. Haven't you been this side of town recently?"

"Not for quite a while. Years prob'ly."

"Oh, well let me give you the guided tour then."

"Really? So, should I be adding tour director to your already impressive list of accomplishments?"

"No, but close. I actually worked at the first holo-park for a couple months outta college. So, I can play tour guide just as well as the best of 'em. Like, coming up on the left you'll have just a spectacular view of New York's first, ultra high-tech forcefield suspension bridge, while on the right, in the distance, and way above the Manhattan skyline, may I direct your attention to the Kings Hotel. The second highest structure in our illustrious city."

"Uh huh, whatever. Save it, Sherlock."

"What? Is that disinterest I hear in your tone. Are you trying to imply, or outright say, that my tour guide skills are somehow lacking?"

"God forbid." She giggled. "It's just I can't really see anything outside at the moment."

"How come? Something wrong with your car's visuals? 'Cause you can use mine, if you'd like."

He popped up on a life-sized air screen in front of her. In very handsome profile, as he sat in his car looking straight ahead through his windscreen. His damp hair shifted a bit in the breeze coming through the open driver side window.

"No…uh, it's actually 'cause I put on the windows' privacy mode while my uh…top dries."

His head jerked to the right, over to her. His gaze collided with hers.

At first.

"Oh crap!" He looked away in the next second, as his proximity alarm sounded, he jerked his steering wheel to the left.

She heard the honking of a horn and a distant expletive.

"Are you okay up there?" She gasped, then giggled, feeling nervous.

"Uh, yeah, I'm good. Oh my gosh, I'm so sorry, Marly. I didn't realize you were…uh…" The right side of his face, that she could see, turned three different shades of red. His knuckles, in contrast, were white, as his fingers gripped the steering wheel.

"No worries. Honest mistake." All thumbs suddenly, she tugged at her blouse and finally got it down from where she had it hanging, over the front seat head rest, and just over the back seat blowers. She held it up to her chest, over her lacy bra. "Maybe we should switch the video off for the time being?"

"Yeah, right. Of course." His gaze snapped back to her for a nano-second, just before he switched off the video feed. "That's pro'bly a good idea. Don't think I could concentrate on the road otherwise…"

She heard his deep, grating inhalation.

Then his even deeper, velvet over gravel voice.
"Like. Wow…by the way…"
He exhaled.
She grinned.
"So, tell me…"

They chatted for just over half an hour more after that, until –

"Okay, we're here. It's just up there on the right."

"Okay cool. See you in a bit."

She'd switched off her privacy setting by then, so she watched as her car followed his as he pulled off the main thoroughfare and into a gorgeous looking development. Admiring the view through her windscreen and side windows, they passed communal 3-D gaming courts, traditional sporting grounds, kids' playground, a huge Olympic sized swimming pool, and club house. By the time they pulled into his driveway, she felt star struck.

"Come on in." With a wave of his hand his huge front door shimmied, phased out, and then disappeared entirely. He ushered her through, and she looked back just in time to see it reform again.

She reached out and touched the solid shiny surface. "Wow."

"I know, right?" He grinned. "Just give me a couple minutes to get changed outta these chilly, wet clothes. The guest bathroom is right through there if you want to freshen up. And I can get you a dry tee-shirt, some sweats, or something if you'd like?"

"Oh, no thanks, I'm fine." She looked up, smiled at him. "The blower in my car did the trick. Warmed me right up. Uh…I mean, it really worked for me."

"I'll say… worked for me too…"

They shared a heated look.

Taking in a deep breath, she walked past him and looked around the downstairs area of his house.

"I don't want to sound like a looky-loo or anything, but it just must be said. Like… OMG…you live here?!" She tried not to gape as she let her gaze roam around a home that rivalled Dani and Joe's in sheer size, and beauty. The only difference was where theirs had classic, old age touches, his was completely new age. Futuristic even.

"I mean, when I saw your Ferrari Sky-Reacher outside on Dani's driveway when we left her house that first night, I just figured it was on lease. But now…" she looked around again. "How in the hell can you even afford all this on a media guy's salary?

"Oh no." She took a step back. "You're not a gold smuggler, are you?"

"What?!" He barked out a laugh and then continued laughing. "You're incredible. You know that, right? No. Ms. Cynic. I'm not into any criminal activity, of any kind."

"Just checking. You can't be too careful 'cause yuh just never know these days."

Similar to the old time Golden Age of Piracy in the late sixteen into early seventeen hundreds, sometime after the defenders arrived, there'd been an upsurge in daring thefts. Only instead of on the high seas, these were happening in midair. Hundreds of hover-vehicle shipments of gold, moving between states and even overseas were being brazenly hijacked by air-pirates in carefully planned and spectacularly executed heists.

"And by the way, that shiny, silver, bad boy on the driveway out there, is all mine. Bought and paid for. The culmination of a shy boy's dream to fly." He grinned and winked at her.

"And is that the model I've read about? The all-terrain one? Even travels on water? And with the stealth tech?"

"Aww yeah."

"That hover-car costs like fifteen mil, shy-boy. So how *did* you afford that, exactly? And like Rissa would say, should we be talking about your net worth, right about now?" She giggled.

"Oh. I just inherited a little money after my parents passed, that's all." He shrugged.

"A little?"

"Okay, maybe more than a little." His smile was sheepish. "But I'd give it all away tomorrow, if it threatened my salvation, or if it meant I could see them both, just one more time."

He looked so sad in that moment; she searched her mind for words that would cheer him.

"Don't you worry, aren't they the reason you're so grounded in your faith?"

He nodded.

"Well, then you will. You'll see them again in the fulness of God's time."

"Yeah, I sure hope so." He gazed down at her

with a soft smile on his face. "Okay," he shook his head, "let me go get changed, then I'll go grab us those treats from the pantry. You take a seat. Make yourself comfortable. Oh, and just say 'movies' to the wall module over there, near to the sofa and it'll bring up a list. Choose whatever you like. But just so you know, I'm feeling rom-com." He rubbed his hands together. "Yeah? Am I right?"

"Good to know, but you can just keep on *feeling* it 'cause we're gonna be *watching* sci-fi here tonight."

She flashed him a cheeky grin.

He gave her a blank look. "Really?"

She shrugged. "And I have to say, I never would have pegged you for a 'chick-flick' kinda guy."

"Say what you like, but 20th and 21st century filmmakers were onto something there, you know. Those movies were quite often just lighthearted depictions of some real-world, deep, emotional relationship issues. Never underestimate the power of a good rom-com, I say. They weren't just entertainment, they were instructive."

"Seriously? Whatever, Newton."

"You know, that reminds me, do you realize that in all the time since we've reconnected you have never ever called me by my first name?"

"Nuh-uh. No way."

"Uh…yes way. It's always Newton, or my full name, or Sherlock, since this morning anyway. Hell, even 'hey you' on occasion. What's up with that?"

"Let's just say if you knew what else I've been calling you in the last few years, yuh woulda been real happy with any one of those."

"Uh-huh…" He shook his head and regarded her as she shrugged and giggled.

"Okay, hang tight. I'll be back." He turned to the wall behind him, pressed a small raised and glowing section, and a large lit square detached from the floor right under his feet. He grasped the shining pillar of light that rose up from its center and the energy platform carried him swiftly and silently to where a section of the upper floor balcony barrier slid open.

He disappeared down a corridor and she sauntered over to the wall unit.

"Movies."

She started flipping through the impressive selection it displayed, and after about five minutes, she settled on one of her favorites, the sci-fi classic, *Avatar*. She'd seen it like ten times already but couldn't wait to watch it again. "Now that'll be good for a couple hours of primo sci-fi action."

"Oh yeah, for real, that's actually a great choice."

She spun at the sound of his deep, and smoothly cultured voice right above her head. And for the second time that night, lost her balance, and then collided–

–with a veritable wall of pure muscle–sheathed in a super thin vest and a pair of soft sweatpants.

"Whoa… Oh, my God…" Her gaze landed on his chest and she lost her breath. She held on as he caught, and steadied her. Then she let him go. Took a couple steps back.

What was wrong with her? She'd been literally waiting for this moment. For his kiss. For four years. Hell, her whole life even. Why, oh why, was she so nervous now?

"You, okay?" His voice was soft, deep, and husky.

Just a heaven-sent, vocal thirst-trap.

"Huh?" Her gaze snapped up to his amused, warm, bronze one. "Oh yeah, uh…didn't realize you were standing right behind me. Wow, your floor is slippery. You should…uh…do something about that. What…? You just startled me, that's all."

"That's all, huh? Come on now, *Marly*, wasn't it you who said you're trying to speak only truths from now on?" His brows rose in challenge.

Uh-oh…

And there it was. His voice. Saying her name. Like *that* again…

Double uh-oh.

"Isn't there…oh, I don't know…something else maybe, you want to say to me?" He took a step forward on silent, bare feet.

"Uh…no. I don't…think so." She took another step back, with a click, in her very favorite high heels, and still, he towered over her.

Anxious and unsure, now that the moment was finally here, she retreated another step.

And then another.

Click.

And dropped.

Right over the low arm of his huge, comfy looking sofa.

Her gasp was as much from the fall as it was because of his next action, as he immediately reached down and rested his palms on either side of her hips. She pushed up and braced herself with her arms behind her. Heard his sharp intake of breath as his brown gaze followed the line of her thighs under her skirt, in a near physical touch, and then ran over her bare calves. He looked over, into her eyes, and exhaled on a slow breath that brushed her knees.

Uncertainty be damned.

She let her shoes drop to the floor and inched back. He noted her action, his mouth turning up in an attractive half smile. Then like a prowling wolf, he followed her down. Closely. Though not touching her as he continued to hold her gaze.

Smiling, she licked her lips as she warmed to their game. She kept easing back, and sure enough, he kept following her forward. At least until her shoulders hit the arm at the other end of the sofa.

"End of the road." He gave her his trademark slow smile, as his hips at last settled beside hers. Balanced on his strong forearms at either side of her head he leaned down, nuzzled her neck. Came back up, with a slight flaring of his nostrils, he looked into her eyes again. "Mmm, you always smell so-ooo good. Makes me absolutely crazy…know that?"

He smiled, dipped his head about halfway, gave her a questioning look, but then pulled back a fraction, just as she nodded and reached up.

"Uh-uh…" He shook his head, the lazy smile still playing at his lips.

Puzzled, she tried again, but still he kept his lips just out of her reach as a slight smile continued to grace them.

"Don't you remember?"

"Remember what?"

"That this is the part where you ask me…

Nicely. So, tell me…What… Do you want, Marly?"

His voice was a seductive rumble.

His gaze. Intriguing.

"Just kiss me, already." Every nerve ending tingling, she could hardly think straight and felt like she was burning up by slow degrees. "Satisfied?"

"Not nearly." His left eyebrow rose slowly.

"Please…" she groaned.

"Please…who?"

Confused, she hesitated.

"My first name… Say it."

"Please…Dax," she breathed.

"Ah…as my lady commands." He lowered his head, and she received a quick, soft kiss on her lips as she met him halfway. He drew back again, smiling as he toyed with her. While she, very nearly screamed in utter frustration.

He lost his smile then… His gaze got intense.

Feral.

"Say it again…"

"Dax."

And she lost her breath, as his head lowered all the way this time, and he joined their mouths in a sudden and voracious exploration.

A kiss, more than worth the wait. For real.

The sound of her breathy sighs joined with his harsh, grating inhalations, as their mouths met and clung. Separated… and came together again. And yet again.

Caught up in the moment, she gripped a handful of his vest at his waist, intending to tug it off him. He placed his hand over hers. Stilled her action as he pulled back a bit, his eyes searching hers.

His voice a grating rumble, he let out a groan that sounded almost pained. "Okay, so maybe we should watch that movie now? Before we don't wanna stop?"

"Forget that… What movie?" Her words came out on a breathy whisper.

"You. Are… Amazing." His gaze roamed over her. Everywhere. Igniting her blood, and in a fog of passion, she pulled him back down to her again. And he heeded her wishes. Devoured her mouth, over and over again, for long…mind and body arousing minutes.

This time when she reached for his vest, he pulled away completely, with a jerk. Sat up on the sofa and gazed sideways at her. His look, still one of super-intense attraction. But now, all rolled up in that absorbing, intriguing intent.

"Yeah, we def need that movie. Like. Right now." He blew out a noisy breath, slapped his powerful thighs. Twice. Then rose with manly grace. Turning in a slow half circle until he was facing her, with eyes closed, he rolled his broad, solid shoulders, and rocked his gorgeous head like he was trying to shake it free, of something.

Sitting up more slowly, she struggled out of her own sensual haze.

This was so completely unlike her, she barely recognized herself.

She had never been anywhere near as physically close to a man like she had with Dax in those amazing, gratifying, intimate moments they'd just shared. Had never felt that way before. Ever.

Such need.

No.

Hunger.

Such a compulsion. A craving to touch. To feel…

His bare skin with her hands, under her fingertips…

To taste him…with her lips…an open mouth…her tongue.

It was far more intense, more consuming than anything she'd ever experienced, in her life. Surprising, for real, and not just because of how much of a departure it was for her, but also because of just how comfortable it felt.

She stared. Got another really good look at him, as he stood before her, only a few paces away. Who knew he'd been hiding a body like his under all those finely tailored business suits

Oh my…

"Just gimme a minute–"

Her gaze snapped up.

Collided.

With his smoky brown, amused one. And a knowing smile.

"…because I'm def gonna need to go wash my face in some really…I mean like *seriously*, we're talking arctic, icy water. In the guest bathroom."

"Uh…you have one of those new ice-bath systems? With the glacial water, I mean?"

"Uh-huh. Just got it installed a couple months ago."

"Okay, really? Great. Uh…for the fat resistance ice treatments like the gym?"

"No. For you…"

Whoa…

"Since we reconnected. Had a feeling I'd be needing it…sooner, or later… Or maybe even sooner." His smile was adorably crooked.

"Oh…okay."

Her heart did a little flip in her chest.

"So, don't move a muscle. I'll be right back."

"Oh yeah, no muscles moving…uh…here," she finished weakly, feeling her face heat. But then contradicted her own words as she scooted down and leaned over the arm of the sofa closest to him. Enjoying that view too, as she watched him stride away.

"And stop watching me walk away, woman." She heard the growl he emitted turn into a deep chuckle, as he disappeared around the corner leading to the downstairs bathroom.

She turned back.

"No muscles moving here? Really?" She slapped a hand to her forehead wondering when she'd become such a complete idiot.

Then grinning, she clapped a hand to her mouth to stifle her shriek of pure, unadulterated delight.

Chapter 20

Psalms 37:4
Delight thyself also in the Lord; and He shall give
thee the desires of thine heart…

It was near daybreak when she arrived home and floated into her apartment, on a high of sheer, unadulterated delight.

She and Dax had barely watched one of their very favourite movies, instead they'd spent most of the rest of the night talking, laughing, and connecting in a way she'd never dreamed possible – on an emotional, intellectual, and all-important spiritual level.

And when she finally left his home, they'd shared only one more long, fulfilling, yet still somehow…not enough, mind-blowing kiss. Outside.

Under the stars. Holding each other. Super close. Pressed together. Chests right down to knees. Well, maybe not knees, since his kinda ended up nestled between hers…

Once he'd pressed her back…up against her car door.

The kiss they should have shared that night she'd learned the truth about him, she thought, and somehow knew he did too, as he matched her fervour with equal and compelling intent. Making up for lost time and so many missed golden opportunities.

Then, when they finally separated, he waved her door open. Firmly, yet somehow still gently, urged her into her car seat, and instructed her to drive away.

While he could still summon the willpower it took, to let her leave.

To watch her get into that car.

Instead of sweeping her up in his arms. Back into his home. And into his bed.

It felt amazing, and enveloping, and crazy, in a good way, and yes, even a little bit scary. But more than all of that, it just felt…

Easy.

And right.

In a phrase – heaven sent.

And after she changed into her pyjamas and prepared for bed, she didn't follow her nightly ritual. She didn't walk on bare feet to her front door. She didn't double check it was locked, or even if she'd remembered to set the alarm. She didn't switch on the passageway light. And she didn't wonder if she'd ever have a normal, decent, uninterrupted night's sleep, ever again.

Because as soon as she arrived and checked her social media, there was just one single message waiting–

Digital Dante

My Lady Cynic, from the very second you left me, I felt your absence, keenly. So, I could think of no better way to express my longing to see you again, than to look to the writings of Dante, for he said this with far more eloquence than I ever could–

"Remember tonight... for it is the beginning of always..."

Till next time, my beloved... I leave with you, for safe-keeping, my very heart... for it...and I...are forever yours. ♥

"So, that's why he didn't call on the ride home." Smiling, she reached over and tapped the com unit on her bedside table. "Call Dax."

"Hey babe, was just about to call. Got home safe and sound?"

The rich, deep sound of his voice filled her room in a whole new way.

"Yep." She hit the button for video and his handsome, smiling face popped up, along with–

Whoa...

His completely bare, and beautifully chiselled torso.

Shoulders. Biceps. Pecs. And a six pack to die for. All filled her vision at once. Every angle, every line. Smooth spots and ridges. Sinks and curves.

Contours and highlights. Shadows and light. Every inch of skin and sinew previously hidden from her. Every pleasure she'd been denied. Revealed. In splendid, God bless the inventor, absolutely glorious, realistic 3-D.

Solid. Extraordinary. Irresistible… Everything she'd imagined that night, and so much more. And all just begging for her attention.

"So, now is when you let me see you like that. When I'm miles away and can't even touch you? Why? Why would you torture me like this?"

His smile was slow…and crazy-good.

"It's safer this way. Trust me."

"Oh, I do trust you. Completely. But safe? Hmmm… What makes you think I want to be safe from you…Dax?"

"Quit poking the bear, woman." He shifted and let out a raw sound that was half groan and half growl.

"Whaaat?"

"Oh, you know exactly what. Quit it."

"It was a simple question, yuh know."

"No. It wasn't. It was a complicated question with an even more complex answer. And one you're not going to be able to handle because you're not ready for my brand of crazy…yet."

"I'll be the judge of that and trust me. I can handle a little crazy. I can handle…*all* your crazy."

He eyed her.

Melted her. With just one intense look.

He breathed in.

Then did that thing. That thing where he closed his eyes and rocked his gorgeous head from side to side. If she were a photographer, or an artist, she'd have wanted to capture him. Just like that.

"Okay… So, I'll come get you later this morning. Around seven? For breakfast at that French patisserie, you suggested earlier?"

"Yuh mean in half an hour?"

They both consulted their watches.

"Oh crap. I completely forgot how late…uh…or rather, early it is," he smiled as she giggled. "So maybe lunch instead?"

"Or brunch? I'm not really that tired."

"Liar…"

She should have been offended, given her truth rule, but the way he said it… made it sound like a racy endearment. A timely reminder of the degree of intimacy they'd shared. Were still sharing, and all in such a short space of time.

"No truly, I feel…energised."

"Really? 'Cause I'm pretty sure this is the fourth night in a row you haven't had a decent night's rest."

"And how would you know that?" As though summoned by his words, she stifled a yawn.

"There, see? My point exactly. Plus, I was with you all night tonight and in the void last night, and when we had our little space odyssey after that, as you may recall. That's two nights right there. Then today, you had on your power suit and those killer heels you like so much. Love the way your legs look in those, by the way…mmm…"

"Yeah? Yuh do?" She felt her face heat at the deep rumble in his voice, and from the way he watched her.

"Aww yeah… like you wouldn't believe. I take

one look and it's like I can feel both of them…and you…wrapped all around me… Uh…so anyway–" he shook his head, cleared his throat, "–Where was I? Oh yeah, I saw the alert come up when we were standing next to your car at Joe and Dani's on Tuesday night. You know, the one with the reminder to research the changes to world policy on thermonuclear and bioweapons disarmament?"

She gasped. "You saw that?"

"Kinda hard to miss a pop up like the one you programmed. Plus, I can read forwards, backwards, and upside down."

"Well, of course you can!"

She giggled as he grinned.

"So, if you'd finished it, you would have pitched the idea to your boss the next day. The way you were dressed means you didn't present your outline till today, or rather yesterday because you were still working on it Wednesday. And because you're such a perfectionist, prob'ly Thursday night too. Am I right?"

She shook her head on a smile, "Can I just say, it's so totally awesome, the way you do that. You are amazing. You know that? I mean, seriously. And so-ooo hot right now. I'm officially turned on, all over again."

"I know, right? Me too…"

Whoa…

"Whoa… Oh my God. Don't do that."

"Do what?"

"You know very well. That thing you're doing…with your eyes. Don't look at me like that." She resisted the urge to fan herself under the weight of his intense and penetrating gaze. Reaching right into her…searching her…touching her.

Everywhere.

"I can't even… You're there and I'm here. It's not fair. And the way I feel… I can't even explain it… It's like I'm burning up… melting… I dunno… I can't take this. This thing between us. It's too much… I just can't take–"

"Oh, yes… yes, you can. And you will… Well… Maybe not all at once…but slow and easy at first, I'm guessing… But then, later…"

He leaned forward… His gaze going from intense, to nuclear.

"OMG… Dax… You have to stop. Right now. I'm serious. Whew!" She made a time out sign with her hands.

"Like I said… My brand of crazy…remember…? And that…was only a sample…"

His smile was a leisurely invitation. Urging her to unconditional surrender.

"Point taken. Enough. Wow…"

It was all in his eyes… The way he looked at her. Saw her. He had the power to transport them both. Like in his dreams. It was like she could see them together in her mind. Feel him… She really did use the neckline and collar of her pyjama top to fan herself this time.

"So, uh… I'm really digging the way that journalistic mind of yours works. Obviously. It's just like you said…uh…yesterday morning at the café. You really are all about it, huh?"

"No… not this time. That was all you, Marly.

For real. I am *all* about… you…"

She felt his gaze touch her. Again. To her core. Their connection reached out, despite the distance. It held her. Absorbing and heated, like a torrid embrace. Yet still tempered with such tenderness.

"I feel that same way too."

They looked at each other. In silence. Enjoying yet another exquisite moment.

"So, brunch? Unless…uh…*you* wanna get some sleep?"

"Sleep? Like hell. Brunch it is. I'll sleep when I'm dead and until the good Lord calls me. In fact, I'd come get you right now, if you want. Just say the word. I'll fire up the jets on the Sky-Reacher and be there in ten. I've already waited too long to spend time with you. I'm not letting us waste another heaven-sent minute."

"I can't wait to see you too… To have you hold me again."

He put a hand up and she held hers up against his. Their fingers entwining in a virtual caress.

"Speaking of which, I read your message, yuh know. Beloved, huh? I think I like the sound of that."

"Yuh do, huh?"

His smile, along with the deep, husky tone of his voice set her heart aflutter. All over again.

"Aww yeah, I like it… A lot."

She grinned.

He chuckled. Lowered his hand, then slowly leaned back in bed. He put a muscled forearm behind his head, his smoky brown eyes hooded.

"What about brunch?" she wondered.

"There's time. Talk to me."

Tucking her legs in under her blanket she settled into hers with a smile.

"Well…speaking of us…both…being in love."

She took a moment. Basked in the warmth of his smile.

"Since you mentioned them last night…I was going through a list of my favorite iconic rom-coms, on the drive home, and it got me thinking…about us…"

Chapter 21

1 John 4:12
No man hath seen God at any time. If we love one
another, God dwelleth in us, and his love is
perfected in us…

They got married two weeks later.

The way Dax put it when he proposed, was that it was like Billy Crystal's Harry said in the poignant ending of the iconic rom-com - *When Harry Met Sally*, "When you realize you want to spend the rest of your life with somebody, you want the rest of your life to start as soon as possible." Or maybe he said, "right away". She didn't really remember because before he'd even finished his touching declaration of undying love, she'd been too busy shouting, "Yes! Yes! Yes!"

Telling him she loved him every bit as much.

And kissing him.

"That was really great, wasn't it? I think it's fair to say that our very first party with the crew was a fabulous success."

"Definitely." He leaned down and pressed a soft kiss on her lips.

It was the middle of autumn, but still quite warm, so they'd decided to have a Saturday lunchtime barbeque instead of a dinner party, about a week after they'd returned from their amazing honeymoon on Mars. Bringing in all the dishes from where they'd entertained their little group of friends outside on the patio, they started loading them onto the kitchen counter.

"And I'll tell you what, that Jamaican barbeque sauce that Joe whipped up was just phenomenal." He picked up some more plates and followed her back into the kitchen. "I mean on everything. I swear if he'd put it on one of the garden hoses out there, I would have eaten that too."

They shared a laugh.

"For real. He needs to bottle and sell that puppy."

He nodded. "I know I'd buy it. Tasted just as good as what I had while I was on the island last year. Okay, come on Sparky," he gestured to the dishes, "let's you and me get all this stuff cleaned up."

"Really? Again, with the Sparky? I know it's from my name, but whenever you say it, I feel like there's more there. So, spill it, why *do* you call me that?"

"Well, I know you'll prob'ly think it's kinda silly, and corny as all hell, but," he pulled her forward and looked down into her eyes, "after we met, from the time we kept butting heads, I just always remember thinking even though we constantly *spar* with each other, you still held the *key* to my heart."

"Aww… Wow babe," she gazed up at him, "that may just be the sweetest thing you've ever said to me."

"Really?"

"Really." She crooked her finger at him and licked her lips.

His smile was slow as his head descended to hers.

She reached up, cupped the side of his face as his eyelids lowered.

Then she pinched his left earlobe.

Hard.

"Ow! What the hell, Marly! Dang!" His eyes flew open wide as his head snapped back up. He rubbed his ear as he winced. "What'd you do that for?" He pulled away a bit as he eyed her.

"Really sweet story… But, still just a very popular name for *A dog*, Newton. Everybody knows that, and I hate it. So quit it. Or the next time you call me that, I'm gonna grab a hold of something that'll be a whole lot more painful than your ear. Yuh got me?" She glared at him.

He looked stunned, then sheepish. Like a little kid caught with his hand in the cookie jar. Then his face broke out in a wide grin.

"Yes ma'am, Mrs. Newton."

"Now that's much better." She mirrored his smile. "And I got you beat, by the way. Bet you didn't know I used to call you Mr. Insufferable." She smirked at him.

"Oh, I actually already knew about that."

She gasped and he grinned.

"What? How?"

"Dani told me. The same day you told her, if memory serves."

"Ooo… I'm never confiding in that little blabbermouth ever again."

"Come on now, all's fair in love and war."

"True, especially since I won."

"Oh, I'd say we both did. Which reminds me. Ouch. That really hurt, woman." He rubbed his earlobe again. "You realize of course you're gonna have to make it up to me later, right?" His voice was like velvet on gravel. He looked at her sideways with a half-smile, as his brows lifted.

"Excuse you? Have you even met me?" She put her hands on her hips and eyed him right back. "Forget later." Holding his gaze, she took two steps back. "Half the reason I did it, was so you'd get all hot…and riled up…just like I want you," she lowered her voice to a husky drawl, raised her right eyebrow. "So…are you? All hot and riled up…like I want you?"

"Yes ma'am, Mrs. Newton." He gave her an intense look that ignited her blood.

And she caught his fire.

Reached out and tugged him towards her. Pulled his hips in close to hers.

"Are you sure? 'Cause I could help with that, yuh know… Oh!" She let out a little shriek as he bent his head low and nipped the side of her neck. Heard his sharp inhalation, as he soothed the sweet hurt with the tip of his tongue, then dragged his parted lips from the base of her neck right up to her ear.

"For a thing desired always brings *such* delight…" He growled low.

"There's my Dante," she breathed, as she met his heated gaze. "Okay…now say it in crazy-sexy French… Dax."

He smiled. And she lost her breath as in one move, he lifted her, wrapped her thighs about his hips, and in two purposeful strides had her back touching the kitchen wall.

She gripped his shoulder and the back of his head, as they locked gazes.

"Car une chose désirée…apporte toujours…" was as far as he got, before she joined their mouths in a fiery exchange.

And as he steadied her…and pressed her back against the wall…

Chapter 22

---

1 Samuel 17:47
And all this assembly shall know that the LORD
saveth not with sword and spear: for the battle is
the LORD'S, and He will give you into our hands…

JAN 20th 2133

"So, picture this, guys… my back's against the wall, right? I can't reach my weapon. Can't even get enough leverage for a proper fist fight. And I'm thinking, if this perp doesn't get the hell on up outta my face, ooo…and push comes to shove… I swear, I'm gonna just reach up and slap the dang taste right outta his mouth. Just like whap-whap-thwack-whack-smack!"

"You're kidding me, right?" Rissa burst into giggles.

"The hell I am."

"OMG! I can't even with you, Dani." Marly roared, as everyone else joined in their laughter.

"So, I see work's still never a dull moment. What about the twins? How are they doing in school?" Rissa asked as her own laughter faded.

"Rissa, girl…too well. Just like their dad." Dani reached over and placed a hand on Joe's arm. "Both of them. They're just too brainy for their own good. They're having some trouble relating to the other kids right now–"

"But, just like me," Joe chimed in, "they'll be fine. The friends and connections worth having will come along at just the right time, bless God. Isn't that right babe?" He winked at Dani, and she giggled, nodded, then leaned forward. He met her halfway and placed a soft kiss on her waiting lips.

"Oh, hell no. Are you two going to start with the inappropriate PDA again 'cause if you are, I swear I'm leaving, before I gag." Marly stabbed her forefinger into her open mouth a few times.

"Uh-uh… Oh, hehll no, Ms. Thing. You've been watching too much 21st century TV again, haven't you?" Dani's lustrous curls bounced on her chest as she shook her head. Her pretty cherry red lips pursed into a cute pucker. "And it's not like you and Mr. Pulitzer prize winner over there are any different." She jerked a thumb in Dax's direction. "Dax, you better get your girl."

They all burst into laughter again.

"Yep, she's got you there, Marly, for sure." Rissa shook her head as she laughed.

"Rissa. I need to speak with you... Come to the kitchen, please."

She froze.

A voice so soft she almost didn't hear it. But she'd know it anywhere.

"Guys, go on ahead, talk amongst yourselves, I just need to check on something in the kitchen. I'll be right back."

She rose from her seat, heard the chatter and laughter continue behind her as she walked the short distance to her kitchen. Heart in her throat, she entered turned right and there he was.

Standing in the middle of the space. Looking exactly as he had all those years earlier.

"Hey Rissa." Blue eyes twinkling, he smiled that same warm and welcoming smile she remembered, like it was yesterday.

"Al? Dear God, it's so amazing to see you!" She launched herself at him and they embraced warmly.

"I never thought I'd ever see you again. Well, this side of heaven, anyway. Must be something serious to bring you here, visible like this."

"I'm afraid it is." He lost his smile.

"Oh God, is it–?"

He placed a gentle hand over hers, where she'd placed it, on her growing belly.

"No." His sincere, bright blue gaze eased her mind, somewhat.

"So, everything's okay in there? You know I'm no spring chicken anymore." She gave a dry chuckle, half meant it as a joke, but then not. Still a little anxious, she awaited his response.

He closed his eyes, took that focused breath that he always did when they'd prayed together. She felt a pleasant tingle in her tummy as his potent blessing flowed through her to the baby.

"He's perfect. You should be very proud." He raised his head and smiled again. "He's going to be an amazing man of God."

She felt rare tears spring to her eyes.

"Seriously?"

"Seriously." He nodded.

She let out a little shriek, they shared a grin, then hugged again. She held on tight, in remembrance, enjoying and absorbing the goodness that was him.

"Okay. Whew…" she blew out a quick breath and gave her head a quick shake as she let him go. "So, if this isn't about the baby, then what?"

He turned to the kitchen door.

It opened and Duncan glanced over his shoulder and backed in awkwardly through the doorway holding a cake box, groceries, and a takeout bag. He held the antique door open with his shoulder.

"Hey babe, you will not believe the day I had. I know I'm late, but I got those Thai appetizers you wanted for the party. And for my best girl, I also got chocolate cheesecake from that place you love. So, basically… I forgive me," he chuckled, as he deposited the cake and the takeout on the nearby counter and turned. He halted and slowly put down the grocery bag. "Who's this?" He raised his chin in Al's direction.

"Wait…" She looked back and forth between him and Al. "You can see him?"

"Yes, Rissa," Al nodded, his face more solemn than she'd ever seen it. "It's time. Time for Duncan and your friends, and soon your world…to know the truth."

He touched the screen in the nearby wall, and it turned on. "You *all* need to see this."

On the floor to ceiling screen was the new US president, sworn in that very day. He was speaking before a large crowd at his inauguration ball.

"What's going on? Who *is* this Rissa?"

She could feel Duncan's anxiety across the space. She went over to him and placed a reassuring hand on his arm, looked deep into his eyes. "I'll explain everything, let's just do what he says and watch this first, okay?" She received his reluctant nod, then went over to the corridor leading to the living room.

"Guys, get in here! NOW!" She moved back over to stand between Duncan and Al who'd just shook hands. She could tell from Duncan's bemused, yet pleased expression, that he'd just been the recipient of Al's trademark, just a touch too much, bliss-filled greeting.

She turned to look at the screen, until–

"We got a problem here, guys?" Dani was the first to turn the corner into the kitchen, her weapon already drawn and trained on Al's head. And she was closely followed by Joe, Dax, and then a wide-eyed Marly.

Right beside his wife, Joe was quick to reach out to the knife block resting on the counter near him. He extracted one of the largest and sharpest ones, then brandished it with remarkable skill. Rissa could see the chef, the surgeon and quite disturbingly – a knife assassin, all come out in him at once.

Dani took her eyes off Al for a nanosecond to wink at him. "That's it, babe, we got this." She glared across the room at Al. "So, what's up?" Her chin popped up in his direction as she unchecked the safety on her firearm.

Buzz.

A thin red laser beam of light extended across the room to a point on Al's forehead.

"Whoa! Whoa! Monzo. Joe." Duncan held up his hands and moved to stand half in front of her and half in front of Al. The pinpoint of light now danced somewhere around his left shoulder.

Al turned, grinning from ear to ear as he wiggled his eyebrows at her.

Now that was the Al she knew and loved. She smiled, feeling comforted that no matter what happened next, they'd get through it. Together. With love and yes, even and especially with humor.

"No need for the hit squad. He's a friend." Duncan extended his arm and placed a hand to Al's back. "Take it easy, guys. And Monzo, that laser gun had better be set to stun."

"Maybe," she shrugged and then grinned as she re-holstered her weapon.

"Geez Joe, and you too? Has she been training you in your down time, or what?"

"Some." Joe shared a grin with Dani as he expertly twirled the knife between his fingers, then deftly stuck it back into the block.

"So, my fellow Americans, suffice it to say, a new era has just begun."

They all turned to look at the screen in the kitchen wall as a familiar voice boomed out.

"No more will we pursue our own interests. The decades of isolationist ideology are over. No more

America first. Instead, we extend our arms to the entire world!" He mirrored his words then paused, as cheers from the surrounding crowd rose up and filled the room for several long seconds.

"Now, I know many of you have been hearing the buzz in underground social media and even some extremist left wing news outlets, trying to falsely discredit and spread misinformation about our defender neighbors. AI generated fake news!"

A chorus of loud booing rose up from the crowd.

"I know, I know." He extended his hands in a call for quiet. "So, I am here to set your mind at ease and to set the record straight. They are now, have always been, and will continue to be the best allies with whom humanity has ever had the privilege to associate. And now, as we move forward to an age of unprecedented global unity. I dare say…universal unity. It will become even more evident, as humans and Verndari… *ALL* come together, under *my* leadership, working side by side to bring about a new world order.

"The time is now, my people."

He looked out into the crowd and then directly into the broadcast camera as he slowly lifted off the ground.

A collective gasp could be heard across the ballroom, and then deathly silence as he rose even higher and then floated forward to the center of the room.

He extended his arms, and the room exploded, in shouts, cheers, and applause.

"Give up your religions, your false doctrine! Believe in me! Come! Join. *Me*!" he shouted over the din. "Kneel. Before me! And I *will* lead you!"

"For I am…your one and only, true Messiah!"

Across the room thousands did as he requested and fell to their knees, heads bowed, even as shouts and applause continued to echo across the large ballroom.

In stark contrast, you could have heard a pin drop, as all who were gathered in her kitchen looked to each other. Faces reflecting a range of deep emotions.

"There have been many. But none such as this. Ladies and gentlemen, meet the current manifestation of the spirit of antichrist." Al's soft-spoken words jarred Rissa from her thoughts, confirming her worst, quiet musing.

She gripped Duncan's arms as he pulled her into a tight embrace, even as Dax reached out to hold Marly, as her eyes filled with sudden tears.

Dani leaned against Joe and put her arm around his waist as he pulled her close into his side. His face grim.

Pulling away from Duncan, she looked around at them all.

"What's all this? No. No, guys. We've been praying separately and as a group for far too long for this defeatist attitude to be an acceptable response. Our God is great, and I have to believe our collective faith has brought us all here together for a reason. Plus, every single trial and triumph we've each gone through has made us more than ready for a time like this.

"So, dry those tears, Marly, we've got work to do now to combat that crazy nonsense we just heard.

Now's the time for us to band together, strength in unity in Holy Spirit, remember? We have to rally. All us people of faith.

"It's here, sure, maybe sooner than we imagined. But hey, I maintain we ARE more than ready. As a dear friend once told me, remember, the battle is already won, settled in heavenly places.

"So, am I right?" Her mind and heart set with faith-filled determination she nodded at each of them in turn. She felt Duncan grasp her hand, and grateful for his reassuring hold, she was reminded that they had other more potent support. They had the Almighty's very best on their side.

"And besides, we have help. Really powerful help." She turned to Al and raised her eyebrows in silent question, and he smiled and nodded.

She extended a hand towards him, "Guys, I want you to meet my dearest friend in this world and the next. This is my guardian angel, Alcindor."

"But you can just call me Al." He looked at Dani and winked.

"Al?" Dani looked confused, and then like she'd just seen a ghost. "Aww hehhll no." She shook her head. "What happened to the little, old guy?"

"Oh, he's still in here," Al grinned and jabbed a thumb at himself, "somewhere."

"And, I'm not alone." He smiled, as in the very next instant Svikari and another person she didn't recognize, materialized in the kitchen.

"Svikari! I knew it!" Dani pumped a fist in the air. "I cannot believe I was right. You're Archangel Michael aren't you." He nodded once, his expression grave. "I knew it, didn't I tell you…" She grinned as she turned to Joe.

"Don't tell me, the GQ-holo guy is actually an Archangel?" Duncan's voice was dry.

"Really, Duncan?" both Rissa and Dani said at the same time. "Jinx!"

Dani reached out a hand to her and they shared a little giggle, in girl's club understanding.

"And Buddy, of course," Marly nodded.

"Who?" Rissa and Duncan both asked.

"Budbringer. We met him when he was a defender press liaison years ago. He helped us with the early resistance movement. Marly and I sort of put two and two together ourselves. From our night travels, we figured Verndari were the fallen angels, and if that was the case, since he was working against them, then that would make him one of God's messengers. We just didn't know which one," Dax shrugged.

"Gabriel, actually," he beamed. "And still very much at your service."

"Yuh know." Dani looked around at each of them. "Is it just me, or have we all been keeping different details of the world's biggest secret from each other? And it looks like we've all had some kinda personal revelation we had to work through before we could get to this point.

"Years ago, I got this sign, just before I surrendered to God's will, and let His transformational power heal me, so I could ultimately reclaim my joy when I got reunited with Joe. I saw these massive stone idols. Intimidating and threatening as all hell, but then they just started to crumble till they were nothing but rubble and dust.

So, it occurs to me, this is just like that. Antichrist, his evil minions, and anyone else who's dumb enough to follow him. They are *all* going down. Mark my words."

"Danielle is quite correct. This next temporary reign of Antichrist on earth was inevitable. Which is why we're onto the next phase in your journey… my dear, dear children of the Most High. Take heart, for He is still upon the throne." Gabriel smiled at each of them in turn.

"Make no mistake. There is war within the ranks of evil as we speak. The father of lies is under constant siege, from all sides. We, God's true messengers, alongside you, and other faithful like you, will now band together as never before and use that internal rebellion against them. I have it on good authority that we'll also soon be joined by a few more precious allies, who will now take the lead. From your team and ours." He touched the side of his nose and grinned. "Together, we will distract, use the ensuing confusion and chaos to our advantage to protect and defend our own. So, as they spend time fighting each other, while still trying to lead souls to damnation, we, who are guided by, and are in full support of our supreme Creator, will win as many souls over to the winning side as will so choose. Over to the side of love, truth, and life. Glorious eternal life, in Him who alone is able to sustain it. Amen?"

"Well, Amen and Amen. Take us to church, Gabriel, that was just a glorious mouthful, wasn't it? And good enough for me. You heard him people and…uh…other angels." Dani nodded. "I'd say it's time to really put our faith to work and see what's poppin'. Are you with me?"

"Yeah. Absolutely. Of course." Every human in the room voiced their whole-hearted agreement.

"That's what I'm sayin'." She reached over and did a double fist bump with Michael.

"Welcome to the revolution, people.

"For real…"

EPILOGUE

"Is she asleep yet?"

"Almost."

"Good. Everything is in place."

"Yes, and the message is clear."

"Like crystal."

"And so simple. Can't believe I didn't see it until the Creator revealed it. His glorious purpose is going to be made manifest in her life, and in the lives of so many others. Like never before."

"The exiles want to invade dreams and use them…then so will we."

"Only better."

"Oh, for sure… Infinitely better. It's on, now."

"Get ready world, because your dreams…"

"Aww yeah…"

"They're about…to get…"

They bumped fists filled with brilliant light.

"Real."

Love is Deborah Lamoreaux's raison d'être.

She lives to immerse her readers in a rich fantasy world where magical faraway places and unwavering fated love all come together to create a delicious, satisfying melting pot of literary distraction.

In her world love is always true, unexpected, undeniable, unconditional and of course… everlasting.

Ms. Lamoreaux only ever comes alive when she's let loose to produce her next work of romantic fiction and each and every time that you journey alongside her, within the pages of one of her creations, she escapes the confines of imagination… So come, escape with her…

Don't miss <u>Surrender</u> and <u>Transform</u>!

9 781965 352748